COUSINS AND CIRC

Is Wales, North Dakota . . . . Lucy friend, Gwin, recently come to it . . . . father, says it is. Her father does not think it is a good place to rear children. Lucy is shocked. And yet it almost seems as if Gwin is right. A baby dies, maybe because the doctor was drunk. The wrong man is arrested in the local scandal and sent to jail. Lucy is worried not only because she loves Wales, but also because that summer she is going to drive to Minneapolis with her parents to meet cousins she has never seen before. Will they think Wales is a terrible place, too?

Yet there are good things: the country fair; the visit of her nearby Johnston cousins; the Stone Age Girls' club that meets in the little stone house in Lucy's backyard; and the chance to help both the mother of the unfortunate baby and the wrongly arrested man.

All through the 500-mile trip to Minneapolis, four days in the Regal, with rain, mud roads, and bad hotels to contend with, Lucy worries. Minneapolis has a lot to offer, but it is Wales she cares for.

Lucy Johnston Sypher was born and grew up in Wales, North Dakota. It was for her grandchildren that she first began to write about her girlhood in a remote prairie village, and most of the stories in her books are based on true events.

In this series:

Cousins and Circuses

Lucy Johnston Sypher

ILLUSTRATED BY RAY ABEL

PUFFIN BOOKS

To All My Family

PUFFIN BOOKS
Published by the Penguin Group
Viking Penguin, a division of Penguin Books USA Inc.,
375 Hudson Street, New York, New York 10014, U.S.A.
Penguin Books Ltd, 27 Wrights Lane, London W8 5TZ, England
Penguin Books Australia Ltd, Ringwood, Victoria, Australia
Penguin Books Canada Ltd, 2801 John Street, Markham, Ontario, Canada L3R 1B4
Penguin Books (N.Z.) Ltd, 182–190 Wairau Road, Auckland 10, New Zealand

Penguin Books Ltd, Registered Offices: Harmondsworth, Middlesex, England

First published in the United States of America by Atheneum, 1974
Published in Puffin Books, 1991
1 3 5 7 9 10 8 6 4 2
Copyright © Lucy Johnston Sypher, 1974
All rights reserved

LIBRARY OF CONGRESS CATALOGING IN PUBLICATION DATA
Sypher, Lucy Johnston. Cousins and circuses / Lucy Johnston Sypher :
illustrated by Ray Abel.   p.   cm.
Originally published: New York : Atheneum, 1974.
Sequel to: The edge of nowhere.
Summary: While events make her prairie village in North Dakota
seem like a wicked place sometimes, Lucy, for better or worse,
accepts it as home.
ISBN 0-14-034551-5
[1. North Dakota—Fiction.   2. Family life—Fiction]   I. Abel,
Ray, ill.   II. Title.
[PZ7.S9847Co 1991]   [Fic]—dc20   90-41422

Printed in the United States of America
Set in Janson

Contents

Cousins and Circuses

A Circus Summer

The last day of June in 1916 was a record-breaking scorcher. The sun blazed down on the little village of Wales, North Dakota, and on the enormous flat prairie all around it until every inch was heated and dried and baked. Not a breath of wind stirred the dust or so much as quivered the stiff leaves on the tallest cottonwood in front of the Johnstons' house.

There were five cottonwoods in all, the only big trees for miles around, and ordinarily they gave a beautiful cool shade. But the temperature was nearly 100, and as Lucy came out the front door, she saw that even the cottonwoods were useless against the burning sun.

"At least it's better out here than in the house," she told herself. She was carrying the dark-blue crockery pitcher for cold well water, and she had purposely come the long way around to avoid the hot kitchen.

"Hurry, Lucy," Mother called from inside the house. "Don't dawdle, or we'll never make the circus."

"I am hurrying—fast as I can," Lucy answered. Then she paused to hold the screen open for her little tan-and-white terrier. "Come along, Topsy. Want a cold drink?" she asked.

Topsy came scuttling out the door and immediately disappeared around the house, her long pink tongue hanging out.

"Lucy!" Mother sounded exasperated. "Lucy! I don't hear you pumping. Those twenty miles to Langdon can take forever."

Lucy quickly followed Topsy out of earshot.

The pump was in the shade of the house, outside the open kitchen window. There it was slightly cooler. But the pumping was hot work, so Lucy purposely let some of the icy water splash on her dark gingham dress and her long black stockings. A girl almost eleven knew better, but anything to cool off. Besides, right after dinner she'd change to white stockings and her best white middy dress for the trip to the circus.

Lucy had never been to a circus. So now she leaned on the iron pump handle and dreamed of clowns and spangles, of elephants and acrobats, of trick dogs and—

"Yip! Yip! Yip!" Topsy was sitting up on her haunches with her tiny front paws hanging over her chest, begging for a cold drink.

"Goodness, Topsy," Lucy apologized, "my head's so full of the circus that I forgot even you."

While Topsy slurped up her water from a rusty pie tin, Lucy set the heavy pitcher on the bench beside the well. She tucked her pale red hair behind her ears and, shading her eyes with her hand, looked beyond the garden toward the back gate. It was time for Father to come home from the bank for his dinner.

There was Father, on time, but he didn't wave to her. Maybe it's the heat, thought Lucy. Heat like this made everybody cross. Then she began to panic. "I'll bet he can't take us to the circus!" she muttered. That made her laugh. Father always called her the family worrier.

She waited until he was very near the door. Then she asked, "Everything all right for the circus, Father?"

"No, my dear," he said. "We can't go. I'll explain." And he went indoors.

Just then Mother came to the open window. "Lucy," she said, "please yell to Amory that dinner's ready. He needs to wash." Poor Mother looked hot. Her face was perspiring, her pince-nez glasses were tilted down the bridge of her nose, and her big coil of dark brown hair was all askew on top of her head.

"Oh, Mother," Lucy objected, "you know Amory never listens to me."

"Well, yell a couple of times—toward his cave, of course." And as Mother moved back to the hot stove, she warned, "But don't you go anywhere near it, Lucy."

Amory and his two best friends were digging a huge pit in the backyard and calling it a cave. He hated to come up for anything.

"Am-o-ry! Am-o-ry! Dinner's on!" Lucy bellowed, with no results. Then she used Father's power. "Father's home, and he's waiting!"

In a few seconds Amory had climbed up the ladder from his cave and dragged the big wooden cover Father had made partway across the excavation. Amory would be twelve next month, but he was almost as small for his age as Lucy was for hers. Otherwise everything about him was different. His hair was redder than hers, his eyes were bluer, his freckles were thicker, and he moved like dynamite.

Two weeks of digging, and Amory, in his black sateen shirt and his old brown knickerbockers, already looked like a miner or an underground gnome. Now he ran toward Lucy, shouting, "When do we leave? We got to get going—don't want to miss anything!" Still talking at full speed, he hustled in before Lucy could tell him what Father had said. Topsy dashed in behind Amory, sure there must be food when Amory moved so fast. Lucy picked up the chilly sweating pitcher and went slowly through the shed into the kitchen.

Mother was carrying the platter of hot beef-and-vegetable stew into the dining room. "Bring in the water pitcher, Lucy," she said. "Your father's ready to say the blessing."

Every meal began with a blessing, but today it was brief. Then Father dished up the stew and gave his bad news at the same time. "I'm sorry. I can't take you to the circus."

Both children let out loud moans before he went on. "The insurance adjuster is coming. The rest of today and all day tomorrow I have to drive him around the country to see the damage from the tornado two weeks ago. I sold the insurance, and now I've got to see that the farmers get their cash."

"But it's the last day the circus is in Langdon!" Amory said. "Phone and tell him you're busy. You promised to take us, so you are busy, aren't you?"

Lucy kept still, partly because Amory could talk faster and louder than she and partly because she was afraid she'd cry.

Mother, trying to cheer them, said, "Never mind,

you've got your trip next month to Lake Minnetonka—a 500-mile drive. Just think of that!"

Ever since last winter Mother had talked about this visit with her father and her two sisters and their families, and she still made it sound exciting. "You'll see my old summer home and you'll go to Minneapolis, and you'll meet all the relations at the Gale reunion on Gale Island and you'll get to know your Aunt Lucy's children, your four cousins from Virginia."

Of course Lucy was excited about the long journey, the four-day drive each way, the nights in strange hotels and the meals in restaurants, the towns on the way and the city and the lake. But secretly she dreaded meeting those four rich cousins from the South.

The Minneapolis relatives she knew—her Grandfather Gale, and Aunt Frances and her son, Gale, a couple of years younger than Lucy. And the two Virginia boy-cousins, not much older than Amory and Lucy—well, she was used to boys. But the two girl-cousins were already young ladies. What would they think of a girl who had always lived in a prairie village? They had always lived in a city house with bathrooms and maids and dinner served at night. They'd probably laugh at her and at Wales.

While Lucy sat brooding about her cousins, Amory was off on a new argument. "Can't you see what this will do to me?" he asked in a pitiful voice. "I'll have to stay down in the cave—a whole day underground, in the dark with only one candle." He made it sound like a cruel punishment, like being sent to a dungeon.

"Oh, the cave—that reminds me," said Father in a new and sterner voice as he looked steadily at Amory. "You didn't tell me, but Mr. Flint did. Their little Morrie fell into your cave yesterday."

"Was he hurt, Harry?" Mother was alarmed.

"Those Flint brats!" Amory said with contempt. "Why doesn't that family move back to St. Paul and stay there. They just don't know how to live in Wales, that's their trouble."

"But you've got to tell me when something like this happens, Amory," Father said.

"Well, you made that cave law yourself about NO LITTLE CHILDREN," Amory argued. "So when Morrie tried to come down, we boys jiggled the ladder—only a little jiggle really." Amory had begun slowly, but he picked up speed. " 'Course it's a very shaky ladder, but we thought he'd hang on. What does that dumb kid do? He falls bang flat on the floor of the cave."

"First we thought he might have hit our big iron kettle," Amory continued, "but it's not even dented." Then Amory's face lit up with one of his wide smiles. "Lucky we didn't have any fire in the kettle. Real luck that was!"

"And what about your friend Jerry's luck? You never told me he fell into the cave and his folks thought he had a broken rib," Father said.

"Oh, that was three days ago. This morning Stan and I sat and watched Jerry do most of the digging, just to be sure he was okay, and he's fine now." Amory looked very pleased.

At this, Father began to laugh. "Glad I'm not one of your best friends, Amory. I had lumbago in my back for four days after I helped you begin digging—I was bent over like a chimpanzee. I'm lucky you didn't put me back to work," Father chuckled.

So it was Mother who gave the scolding. "What a way to treat your friends, Amory." Amory bent down to his third helping of stew.

Lucy had eaten almost nothing. She was too disappointed. When Father noticed, he began listing all the things that would replace the circus. "Look here," he began, "you've got so much excitement in the next few weeks that I wonder how you'll get it all in."

Father was wound up. "In a couple of weeks the traveling Chautauqua is coming to town again, putting up that big tent on Main Street. Remember how much you liked those programs last summer? That slide lecture and the concert and the play?"

Amory was trying to see how much of Mother's red currant jelly he could pile on one slice of bread and butter, but he paused long enough to object. "You can't sell me on Chautauqua. All ed-u-ca-tion-al garbage. And having it in a tent doesn't make it a circus either."

"Amory, I loved that play—I loved it!" For a moment Lucy forgot the circus in her enthusiasm. "That smiling villain and that innocent man kept in a prison until his girl saved him. It was better than a story in a book! And all the women wore such beautiful dresses and all the men were so handsome. Why, I could see the same play right over again."

"You would like that dopey play," Amory said. "All about love and kisses. Remember how loud they kissed?" Amory smacked his lips against his arm so it sounded like a burst pipe.

"They just kissed once—didn't make any sound at all!" Lucy protested. "And that lecture with slide pictures of New York and Chicago, you said yourself that was good."

"Well, you can go if you like that boring stuff. I'm not going this year." And Amory packed the bread and toppling jelly deftly into his mouth.

So Father tried another circus substitute. "There's

the county fair in Langdon later on in July. You're going to that with your Johnston cousins. And the fair midway is almost a circus, with booths and sideshows, and this year there's an airplane."

Lucy brightened when she thought of a day at the fair with her five Johnston cousins. They were the children of her father's brother, Uncle Charlie Johnston. Since they lived only twenty miles away, she saw them often—to her they were more like four brothers and a big sister than like cousins.

Amory sat grumpily chewing his bread and jelly. Father saw that the Chautauqua and the county fair weren't enough for Amory.

"Next Tuesday's the Fourth of July. Did you forget that, Amory?" Now Father began to sound excited. "I've ordered almost a circus of fireworks—sparklers and giant crackers and twirling snakes and blazing balloons. A whole crate of fireworks!"

At that moment, Mother brought in two outsized rhubarb pies. She heard the word *fireworks* and began to sputter like a Roman candle herself. "Why, Harry," she began as she set the pies down, "you never told me you'd ordered all those fireworks again this year, even those burning balloons to drift all over the prairie? Really—at your age!" Mother thought fireworks were a waste of money and a weakness in Father's character.

"Well, Amory likes—" Father never finished the sentence.

"Amory! Fiddlesticks! You like them quite as much as he does," Mother snapped.

"Oh, rhubarb pie!" Amory changed the subject before Mother could ban the fireworks, and he began to wheedle, "Couldn't I please take one pie—or even half a pie—out to the cave to share with Stan and Jerry?"

Before Mother could answer, someone knocked on the front screen door. Topsy ran to the porch, barking. Mother nodded to Lucy to see who it was. There stood Mrs. Flint, looking very hot in her Sunday hat and her lavender afternoon dress. All the other women wore gingham dresses and aprons until the dinner dishes were done. And only Mrs. Flint would come to the front door. Everyone else in town came to the back one.

In her hand Mrs. Flint held a little girl's pink dress, one of her Dorrie's fluffy, ruffly city dresses, though now it looked as though it had been pulled through a machine.

"I won't come in, Lucy," said Mrs. Flint in her prim way. "I just want to say that Amory and his friends tore half the ruffles off my sweet Dorrie's dress this morning."

"Oh, I'm sure they didn't do that," Lucy said, and then she realized she shouldn't contradict.

"Gracious me!" said Mother, as she came to the door. "I can't believe that Amory would be so rough with a five-year-old girl!"

Mrs. Flint didn't even answer Mother. She just shook the ruffled dress in Mother's face as proof of the crime. Lucy saw that all the back rows of ruffles hung down in streamers.

"Amory," Mother called. "Amory!"

Amory appeared at the door beside Mother and Lucy. "How do you do, Mrs. Flint," he said very politely.

Just like him to try to soft-soap her, thought Lucy.

Mrs. Flint was so angry that she said nothing, only shook the torn ruffles.

"Oh, that must be your Dorrie's dress," Amory stated calmly. "We three boys found her leaning over our cave this morning. And I do think, Mrs. Flint, that we saved her life. We pulled her back by her skirt. But how could we know that those flimsy ruffles were only pasted on?" Amory smiled sweetly.

Mrs. Flint began to say something that even Amory guessed was not a thank-you for saving Dorrie's life. So he raced on. "Did Dorrie tell you—I'll bet she didn't— that she scratched Stan's arm so bad that I just wonder if he might get blood poisoning. You can get it from a cat scratch, you know. And Stan said she scratched like a wildcat."

Mrs. Flint had met her match. Her eyes were popping and her mouth was wide open, ready to say something harsh. But slowly she closed her mouth and turned toward the gate, saying to Mother as she left, "I only wanted you to know, Mrs. Johnston, that your yard is no longer a safe place for little girls." And off she went, through the front gate and along the road, the hot roundabout way back to her house, but the proper way if you had paid a social call.

Back at the table, Father was laughing into his napkin. "I know, I know," he said to Mother, as he put his napkin down. "I should have talked to her, but you three were handling it so tactfully that I thought I might only irritate her." When that excuse didn't work, he said, "It's no use, Caroline. Mrs. Flint comes from St. Paul, and because we live happily in Wales—"

"She thinks we're country hayseeds!" Lucy finished his sentence for him, and wondered if that was what her city cousins would think of them too.

"Anyway, I didn't make that cave law about NO GIRLS, so none of it's my fault," Amory said.

"Hold on," said Father. "Pretty soon you'll be saying that I jiggle ladders for little boys to fall into caves and that I pull ruffles off little girls' skirts. Now let's hear no more of this, except for one thing, Amory. One more accident in that cave, and I'm having Bill Bortz bring his horses and scoop shovel and fill it in—every inch of it."

"You wouldn't!" Amory was horrified. "You couldn't! After all that digging?"

"I wouldn't want to," Father assured him, "but everybody at our place obeys the law, even if it's only cave law. And don't you forget it."

Then Father changed his tone. "Caroline, shouldn't we tell them now about that secret in your father's last letter?" When Mother nodded, Father went on. "You missed the circus today, but your Grandfather Gale has tickets to take you two and his five other grandchildren next month to—guess what?"

"Tell us—right now, and don't tease," begged Lucy.

"To the Barnum and Bailey circus in Minneapolis."

"To the biggest circus in the world?" Amory almost shrieked.

"Three rings to watch at once?" Lucy could hardly imagine it.

"Yes, indeed," Father said. "And now I'll have no more bellyaching about the circus you've lost today. You have the Fourth of July and Chautauqua and the county fair and the biggest circus in the world—all in the next few weeks." Father rubbed his hands as he always did when he was especially delighted. "This will be a circus summer if ever I saw one!"

Under the Cottonwoods

Amory grabbed the tin of rhubarb pie and bolted out the back door to tell the boys. Father pushed back his chair and prepared to leave. "Caroline," he said, "when I go off for all day tomorrow, why don't you and Lucy come along?"

"I wish I could," Mother said, "but tomorrow I have to give two piano lessons. Why not take Amory? Then we can seal up the cave for a few hours, and I'll have a peaceful day."

"Good idea," Father replied. "He can take along his BB gun. Out on the prairie he's less likely to shoot someone."

Mother held her tongue. She didn't like any guns, even BB guns.

As Father left to drive the Regal out of the barn, he

called, "Better lock the driveway gate, Caroline. Schelers' cows are loose today."

So Mother went out the front door, Lucy tagged along beside her, and Topsy tagged along beside Lucy.

Under the cottonwoods Father stopped the auto. "So much went on at dinner that I forgot two things," he said to Mother. "First, when I go near the Morgan farm tomorrow, I want to take some magazines to that young chap, Luke Morgan. I've told you about him. He's turned eighteen now, so he's no longer a ward of his uncle, and I wish he'd go back to Canada. One winter with that Morgan bunch is enough. His uncle, old Morgan, is crooked as a corkscrew."

"And he uses a corkscrew to open whiskey bottles in his blind pig, right here in Wales," Lucy chimed in.

"Yes, Luke stays out at the farm, but I'd hate to see him mixed up in the Morgans' shenanigans," Father said. "Canada doesn't have prohibition like North Dakota, so Luke may not even realize how illegal that blind pig is. Old Morgan could be jailed for it."

"I'll go right in and tie up some *Saturday Evening Posts*." Mother started for the house.

"Wait—the other thing," Father went on, "is that Pete Dickerman tells me that yesterday he moved his family to the old Scott house behind us. Send Lucy over with some of your baking."

"The same Dickermans who lost a little boy with infantile paralysis last August?" asked Mother. When Father nodded, she said, "Oh, dear, I can't forget their beautiful little blond girl, Hilda, crying and crying at the funeral."

"Same hard-luck family," Father answered. "Pete says Mrs. Dickerman still grieves so much that he thought she'd be better off in town. Another baby on the way, too. And he had those twin boys with him, about five or six, I'd guess they are."

"Not two more boys to live on our block and fall into Amory's cave!" Mother exclaimed.

"Yes, and there's a smaller one behind them." Father grinned. "Just you wait until they all fall into the cave at once, Mrs. Johnston. Won't that be an event!"

Then he put the Regal into gear, honked the horn for Lucy to swing open the driveway gate, and waving to the three of them, he drove off in a swirl of choking dust that made the hot, dry air even more disagreeable.

Mother and Lucy stood a moment in the shade of the biggest cottonwood. Then Mother checked the snap lock on the gate and, taking Lucy by the hand, led the way into the house.

"Lucy, my dear, after I phone Sarah Lowenstein to come for her lesson after all, you call the Owen girls to bring their sewing for the afternoon, and then while they're coming take some cookies over to the Dicker-mans. Later on, I'll make a big jug of cold lemonade, and I've dozens of fresh sugar cookies." She put her arm around Lucy. "It's not exactly a circus, but you four girls shall have a party under the cottonwoods."

Lucy wasn't fond of errands or of strangers, and she had her doubts about that beautiful little blond Hilda Dickerman. But Mother didn't give Lucy a moment to beg off. "You needn't stay," Mother said. "By the time you get back, the Owens will be here."

Mother handed Lucy the heaping plate of sugar cookies, and Lucy set out around the block on the dusty road. The old Scott house seemed run-down and shabby even for Wales. It badly needed paint and new boards to mend the rotting front steps. Around in back, the yard was so weedy and littered with rusty cans and old bottles and broken pieces of machinery that Lucy wondered how it could ever be a place for a garden to grow or for children to play.

Almost the moment Lucy rapped on the back screen door, it opened and a very small white-haired boy, dressed in only his undershirt, came running out. Rushing to catch him was a girl about nine years old with long blond braids flying out behind her. By a quick jump Lucy saved the plate of cookies from the ground. Then she watched the girl grab the laughing baby.

And he was really only a baby—not yet two years old, Lucy guessed, and beautiful enough to be a little girl. With his silky silvery hair and his big blue eyes, he was even more beautiful than his sister, who must be the "beautiful Hilda."

"Are the cookies for us?" Hilda asked at the same time she was hugging her little brother and yanking down his too-short undershirt.

"Yes, my mother sent them over," Lucy explained. "My father knows your father. We're the Johnstons, and I'm Lucy and we live over there. That's our barn."

As Hilda turned to look where Lucy pointed, the baby boy almost escaped from her arms again. "Karlie, don't!" Hilda scolded. "You can have a cookie right now if you'll be good," and she stuffed one in his mouth. Then to Lucy she said, "Ma's sick again and Pa had to go to Langdon on the train, so he took Rudolph and Adolph—they're the twins, you know, and they can still ride free. Anyway I had to stay home to watch Karlie and—" Here Karlie almost got away again, but Hilda bribed him with another cookie.

"He's handsome, but he's a handful, isn't he?" said Lucy.

"Yah, he's into everything," Hilda agreed, "but he's

my Karlie. I've took most of the care of him, cause Ma can't do it." Then gripping Karlie tightly by the arm and lifting the plate of cookies high out of his reach, Hilda stepped inside the battered screen door. Yet, in watching everything, she also remembered her manners. "Thank your ma. It was real good of her."

"Come over when you can," Lucy invited her, "and bring Karlie along. And I hope your mother gets better." Going back around the block to her own house, Lucy thought Hilda might not be so bad after all, and she certainly could do a lot of things. At least she made another girl around, and that was something. Before the Owens came in the spring, there hadn't been any girls the right age in Wales at all.

As soon as Lucy was back in her own yard, she saw the three Owen girls and their brother coming along the back walk, Gwendolyn, the oldest, firmly clutching Edward's hand. Each girl was carrying her sewing in a small oval grape basket, which Mr. Owen had painted in a different color for each one. Though the three girls were in dark gingham dresses and long black stockings like Lucy's, Edward was in a pale blue sailor suit, long pants, white braid, and white neckerchief.

"Oh, that Edward," Lucy muttered to herself. "He's all rigged out in one of those English suits again. We'll have to spend all afternoon keeping an eye on his clothes."

Gwinyth, the middle girl, who always wanted to know everything about everybody, shouted, "Lucy, what happened about the circus?" And even in the heat, she ran ahead to get the news.

"Wait till I get my sewing basket, and I'll tell you," Lucy shouted back.

In the shade of the cottonwoods they spread out an

old khaki blanket and unpacked their baskets of pincushions and small scissors and half-finished dolls' clothes. Only Guinevere, the youngest, still played with dolls, but Mrs. Owen, who made every stitch of clothing her family wore, was teaching them sewing as they made whole wardrobes of dolls' featherstitched underwear, dresses, aprons and capes. Lucy had designed and sewed a whole wardrobe to fit her favorite lady doll, Clarissa.

"About the circus—you haven't told us, Lucy. Why aren't you there?" Gwin asked.

Lucy explained, and Gwendolyn said, "What a pity!" A year older than Lucy, though in the same grade at school, Gwen was the Owen ugly duckling, but she was Lucy's favorite. They read the same books, laughed at the same jokes, and dreamed the same daydreams. So when Gwen said, "What a pity!" she truly meant it.

"Probably just a ratty little show anyway, not worth going to," said Gwinyth, who always said whatever came into her head, as though her long brown curls and her wide blue eyes allowed her to say what she pleased. She never read Lucy's books, but she loved Topsy almost as much as Lucy did. So Lucy forgave her everything.

"Once when we still lived in Canada," said eight-year-old Guinevere, "we went to a big circus, but Gwin peeked under a sideshow tent to watch the hula dancers, so Papa took us all home, right away."

"Hula dancers?" Lucy asked. "What's a hula? Did you see one too, Gwen?"

"Goodness, no! I wouldn't go peeking under a tent the way Gwin did." Gwen spoke severely. "Papa said any kind of dancing is a sin, and for Gwin to peek was a kind of sin too, especially since she's in a minister's family. So we'd all just better forget about those hula dancers in the sideshow."

"Well, I won't forget them," Gwin protested. "And now Guinnie's tattled to Lucy, so I'll tell all I please." She sat up straight. "Hulas are women with no clothes on except some hay tied around their middles, and they wiggle all over."

Before she got any further, Gwen shouted her down. "Gwinyth Owen! Hay isn't enough to cover anyone's middle. And you did spoil the circus for the rest of us. Now you keep still." Gwen leaned back against the tree trunk, exhausted. And Gwin, happy-go-lucky Gwin, looked peeved. She even stopped stroking Topsy.

Lucy had never heard the Owens quarrel or even sharply disagree. Must be the awful heat today, she decided. She dropped the subject of hulas at once, but she did wonder if all circuses had dancers dressed in hay.

Soon it was so hot that they all laid aside their sewing, feeling half-asleep. Lucy and Gwen leaned against the rough cottonwood bark, Gwin sprawled with Topsy at the edge of the blanket, and Guinnie sat slowly turning the pages of a volume in Mother's old series of Dotty Dimple books.

"Lucy," Guinnie asked as she looked up from the worn little book, "did you ever have loads of money and live in a big house in a city like Dotty Dimple?"

"Of course Lucy didn't," Gwin answered sharply. "Wales is the only place you know, isn't it, Lucy?" Gwin was still stung by being told not to talk. "Our Great-aunt Maud Guinevere is rich and lives that way in Canada, doesn't she, Gwen?"

"Yes, and so did Lucy's mother when she was little, didn't she, Lucy?" Gwen was trying to make Lucy feel better about knowing only Wales.

"And next month when we drive to Minneapolis,

I'll see my four cousins from the South, and they live that way," Lucy boasted, though she always felt uneasy when she thought of them and compared their life to hers.

Gwin was no longer listening. "Oh, I itch so! I've got terrible prickly heat," she complained, and she clasped and unclasped her hands so that her fingers would rub each other. "Look, Lucy, between my fingers I'm all little blisters."

Lucy leaned over, and at once she diagnosed the blisters. "Prickly heat—nothing! That's just regular prairie itch." Lucy might not know anything about city life, but on prairie itch she was an expert.

"Prairie itch? It sounds awful! Will it be gone tomorrow if the weather's cooler?" Gwin asked.

"Oh, no!" Lucy was very definite. "Mother can give you some of her sulfur ointment that helps, but I've heard folks say—" here Lucy paused for emphasis, "that it can last for seven years."

"Seven years? You can't mean seven?" Gwin burst out. "This prairie! What a dreadful place to live!"

Once more they all fell silent. The only sounds came from inside the house, where Sarah Lowenstein was pounding out scales. In the backyard Amory, Jerry or Stan occasionally came up from the cave to empty a pail of dirt. Otherwise the whole village was as silent as the four girls. Not an auto, a buggy or a wagon had gone by the house for nearly an hour.

After a time the scales stopped. The three boys climbed out of the cave to rest in the shade of the barn. For days the girls had watched the three boys emptying dirt from their shoveling, but because of the cave law, NO GIRLS, they knew only that the cave was now large enough to hold the three boys and deep enough for them to stand upright. And that was all they did know.

Amory now stuck two sharp sticks in the ground, each with a small shingle tacked to it. On both small shingles were big black crayoned letters, but the girls were too far away to read them.

Gwin was the first to suggest action. "Guinnie, you're only eight, so no one would mind if you just tiptoed over and read what's on those shingles," Gwin coaxed, looking at Lucy for agreement.

"It's okay, Guinnie, if you don't talk to them," Lucy said.

So Guinnie closed her Dotty Dimple book and slowly paced toward the cave, the boys watching her every move. She stood in front of the signs for a full minute. Then she came back to the girls with a puzzled look.

"What do the signs say? You can read, can't you?" Gwin asked impatiently, lifting her curls from the back of her neck and flapping them to and fro to cool herself as she waited.

"One's easy," Guinnie reported. "It says THE CAVE MEN. But I can't read the other. Must be in German or something," and Guinnie sat down again.

"Not German," Lucy said. "Amory only knows the German for *milk* and *bread* and *butter* from when Father was teaching us German at breakfast." Then she hastily added, "Of course that was before the war began," for she remembered that it was now 1916, and to Canadians the Germans were the enemy Huns.

"Shall I go see what it says?" Gwin volunteered.

This roused Gwen to a firm "No, Gwin. Don't you go poking your nose into the boys' doings."

So Gwin egged on Guinnie again. "Take this scrap of a bookmark and copy the letters—just as they are,"

Gwin said, giving Guinnie a little shove to start her off.

After a couple of minutes Guinnie returned with this on her paper:

NO WO

MEN ALL

OWED

Gwin grabbed it and read it aloud, just as it looked: "*No Wo Men All Owed.* But that doesn't make any sense. Must be a puzzle," and Gwin turned it around and around. Finally she said, handing it to Gwen, "I thought *woe* had an *e* on the end."

Gwen took one look and exclaimed, "What do you think of that! They're warning us, NO WOMEN ALLOWED. As though we'd want to go down in their dirty old hole." Gwen almost snorted.

"Well, I'd like to go down—just once," Gwin said. "And some fine day I will! I'll climb right down in and have a look-see."

A Rough Wicked Little Town

Lucy, what do you think about boys?" Gwin broke
a long silence.

"What do I think about boys?" Lucy repeated the
question as though she weren't sure what Gwin was
talking about. "Why, I don't think much about them
at all." The heat had so slowed her mind that it was a
full minute before she continued.

"Well, about boys," Lucy began, "I suppose there are
too many of them, around here anyway. We four girls
are almost the only girls our age in the village. And instead of a sister, I've got Amory, and all my cousins
near my age are boys, too. So I wish—I wish all the boys
I know were girls."

"My papa thinks it's too bad there are so many boys,
too," Gwin said. "Papa said it was too bad this village

has so many boys because they'll all come to some bad end, and—" Gwin paused to catch her breath and hastened on. "And he's glad we'll probably move again next year so our Edward won't have to grow up here."

By now the three other girls were staring at her, Guinnie startled out of her Dotty Dimple story, Gwen horrified, and Lucy both shocked and angry.

"The boys in Wales will not all come to a bad end!" Lucy yelled rudely. "Not Amory, not Jerry, not Stan, and how could your Edward that just had his curls cut off and hasn't finished the first grade—how could he come to a bad end in Wales?" For the first time, Lucy was furious with an Owen.

Guinnie looked up round-eyed. "What's going to happen to our Edward? And where is he now?" Edward had wandered off, and the girls had entirely forgotten him.

"Ed-ward! Ed-ward!" Gwen leaped to her feet. "We've got to find Edward." She first scanned the backyard and then she turned to stare across the road.

There was Edward in the field, high on the heap of broken timbers and splintered rafters that had been a creamery until a tornado had hit it early in June.

"Edward Albert Christian Owen! You'll get dirty, and you'll get hurt, too." Gwen dashed through the gate, across the road and up on the pile of smashed wood. Quickly she led Edward down and back into the yard, all the time both scolding and soothing him, and looking quite scared herself.

"Now Edward, you can stay here with us or go play in the tall weeds by the barn, but you stay off those rickety timbers," Gwen said. "Don't go near the cave, either, or the big boys will tease you and call you the Prince of Wales—and you always cry when they do that." Poor Edward, Lucy thought. Being named Edward Albert Christian for the royal Prince of Wales made life difficult in Wales, North Dakota. But he just made a face at the girls and set off for the patch of tall weeds.

Gwen settled back on the blanket, shaking her head. "I don't know what's got into our Edward since he had his curls cut off. He never used to go in dangerous places."

"It's not because his curls are cut," Gwin replied. "Our Edward's changed because he lives in Wales. You know very well, Gwen, what else our papa said about this town." Gwen motioned to stop her, but she went right on. "Papa said, 'This Wales is a rough wicked little town.'"

Lucy could stand no more. "Gwinyth Owen, don't you dare call my home a rough wicked little town." Lucy spoke so loudly that Topsy flattened her ears. "Besides," Lucy continued, "Wales isn't a town. It's a village. And I'll bet your Canada isn't all heaven, either. And if you please, what does your papa think is so wicked about Wales anyway?" Lucy stared daggers at Gwin.

By this time Gwin was also angry. "You can't say Wales isn't wicked, Lucy Johnston. You've just never been to civilized places. They're different."

"Wales isn't wicked just because it's different. It's not! I know it's not!" Lucy refused to give in.

"It is too a wicked town," Gwin said. "It's not only the butcher who gets drunk a lot of the time. It's the only doctor in town too. And worst of all, I'll have you know, my papa saw the priest at a wedding supper the other night, and he had a mug of beer in his hand. He did! He really did!"

"That's not a wicked crime," Lucy argued. "And my father says when Catholics are in trouble, Father Bronowski is the best priest they've ever had here. He cares!" Lucy paused, wondering how she could excuse the doctor. Then she remembered Father had said the doctor's drinking was like an illness. "And Dr. Carmer —well, he needs to go to a hospital and be cured."

Gwin shot back with, "And what do your folks say about breaking the law? How about the Morgans' blind pig, right there behind the livery stable? Everybody knows about it."

That was a clincher, for Lucy knew that her folks thought the blind pig was a disgrace. There old man Morgan and his two sons sold not only beer but whiskey that they brought across the border from Canada, and they sold it to boys as well as to men.

"A blind pig?" little Guinnie asked as she moved nearer. "Poor little pig. What blinded it, Gwin?"

Gwen tried to quiet her with a severe, "Never you mind."

"I'll tell you, Guinnie. It's a place where they sell alcohol to drink, and it's against the law in this state." Gwin didn't stop there. "And I heard Papa say he's written the sheriff to come up from Langdon and arrest every man at the blind pig and shut them up in jail. That'll fix them!" gloated Gwin.

This gave Lucy a new argument. "If your papa has all those men jailed, who'll earn the money to feed the children?"

Gwin was silent for a moment, then she made one more comment. "Yes, the poor children! Papa says another thing that's so wicked around here is that no one cares about the children. They work them, but nobody takes care of them."

Gwen began to move toward Gwin, her hands spread out as though she were about to strangle her; Lucy felt she could do the same. Yet, even in the midst of her anger, Lucy felt a small prick of doubt. She hadn't been to other places. Was Wales a rough wicked little town? Perhaps other places were good places, and she didn't know any better.

Luckily Mother appeared at that moment with a tray of tall glasses of lemonade and a plate of cookies. "Here you are, girls," she said. "You share with Edward, and I'll put the food for the cave at the back door." Soon they heard her calling, "Amory, Amory—cold lemonade. Come and get it."

The girls ate and drank in a moody sort of way, entirely unlike any party they'd had together before. Gwen tried to smile at Lucy, and Lucy tried to smile back. Gwin concentrated on Topsy, feeding the dog bits of cookie each time Topsy sat up and gave her little yipping "Please!" It was as though Gwin wanted to apologize, but couldn't do it to Lucy, only to the dog.

Gwen had to leave early to help her mother. So when the lemonade was gone, she and Lucy went upstairs together so Gwen could choose another Alcott book to reread. Then they walked together to the back gate.

"It's Gwin's prickly heat or her itch or whatever it is that makes her so prickly today," Gwen said. "Really and truly, I love living here, and it's you and your folks that make it a good place to live."

Going indoors to set the supper table, Lucy thought about Wales. Surely it couldn't be all that bad if Gwen liked it. But the blind pig—that was against the law and wicked. No arguing could set that right.

The other Owens were still out in the yard, and Jerry and Stan had gone home when Amory brought in the lemonade glasses from the cave. He had barely stepped into the kitchen when they heard shrieks and bellows. Amory dropped the tray on the nearest chair and darted out. Lucy rushed after him, but Mother stood stock-still, saying only two words, "The cave!"

It was the cave all right. The shrieks came from deep down in, and as Amory and Lucy arrived at the opening, Lucy had one good look into the murky pit. Then she ran screaming back to the house.

"Mother! Mother!" she yelled as she ran. "Amory's cave is full of Owens—it's crawling with Owens!"

"With worms?" Mother yelled from the doorway.

"No—with Owens!" Lucy shouted. By now she was beside Mother, but she still screamed at the top of her lungs. "Gwin and Edward are at the bottom, and Guinnie's partway down the ladder, and on top— Oh, Mother, it's too awful!" Lucy couldn't go on.

Mother shook her by the shoulder. "Lucy, tell me! Are they all terribly hurt?"

"I don't know, Mother." Lucy had begun to sob. "But the awfullest is that Mr. Owen must have come over to call them home, and he slipped in too! Oh, whatever will he think of Wales now?" All Lucy could think was that now Mr. Owen had one more proof that Wales was a rough wicked little town.

At that instant Father honked the horn at the front gate. Mother, instead of moving toward the door, sat down on a kitchen chair. "Lucy, I can't," she said. "I simply can't. You go open the gate, while I catch my breath."

Lucy wiped her eyes as she ran out. She swung open the gate, slamming it tight after the Regal was in the yard. She hoped to keep Father from noticing too much if she asked him a question right away. "Was it a good trip, Father? Did you see a lot of tornado damage?" But Father had already driven in until he was beside the cave.

"Tornado damage!" barked Father. "What's the damage going on here? Who's fallen in now?" In one glance he'd seen the whole disaster. There was no use in pretending nothing had happened.

"Oh, Father," Lucy wailed, "this time it's nearly every Owen in town!" And they saw Mr. Owen's small bald head emerge from the cave, followed by the rest of Mr. Owen, as muddy as if he'd rolled in a mud puddle. Then an equally muddy Guinevere climbed out. Last came Gwin and Edward, both of them not only muddy but smeared with a sticky pinkness.

Could it be blood? Lucy thought in panic. Owens half-killed in her own rough village, incurably wounded

perhaps, or having to lose arms or legs or— In a matter of seconds she thought of enough calamities to last a lifetime.

Already Amory was loudly apologizing to Mr. Owen. "I was just coming back to cover it, Mr. Owen. Honest I was. And it's too bad your kids fell in my mother's rhubarb pie. We boys were saving it for tomorrow

morning when we got hungry."

The rhubarb pie! Of course! Lucy relaxed. Gwin and Edward would live—to explore more of the rough wicked little town of Wales.

Later at supper, after everyone had apologized to everyone else, and Mother had given Gwin a jar of sulfur ointment for her prairie itch, Amory began arguing with Father. "It's not my fault. They all just try to fall in—stupid kids."

But Mother reminded him of Mr. Owen, "You can't call the Methodist minister a stupid kid, Amory. That won't do."

"Well, he behaved like one," Amory replied. Then he looked to Father. "You won't have the cave filled in because a whole family lands in Mother's pie, will you?"

"Amory," Father broke in, "talk sense. You left the cover off, and you know that's against the cave laws. But this once I'll not have it filled in. I'll close it for one day—for tomorrow." Not waiting for Amory to complain, he continued, "I'm taking the adjuster out beyond Rush Lake—almost to Sarles—and I'll drop you off to practice with your BB gun. Then we'll pick you up on the way home."

Amory began to plan. "How about taking Jerry and Stan too?"

"Not a single other boy." Mother laid down her own law. "I'd worry every blessed minute you were gone."

In the evening Father and Amory shoveled out the excess pie from the bottom of the cave. Then together they securely fastened the cover across the top. Lucy and Mother watched from the kitchen window.

It was while Lucy was staring outside that she had her brilliant idea. Surely all the bad temper and trouble today came from the girls being so hot, and without a hideout of their own.

There, not far from the cave, was the tiny stone house where extra coal was stored in the winter. Stones were so rare in North Dakota that when some were left after the house foundation was finished, they had been cemented together into a little stone house.

In summer it was empty. If it were cleaned and the girls moved into it, what a wonderful hideout it would be!

As soon as Father came back in, she asked him, "Father, can't we girls have the stone house for our clubhouse?" She rattled on, while he stood smiling at her. "Can't we, please? Girls do need a hideout as much as boys do."

Father, being Father, didn't say "Yes" right away. But he did begin to tease her so she knew he had decided on a "Yes." "Well, I wonder," he began to drawl. "Girls should have what boys have. That's a good point. But you'd all turn black from the coal dust—blacker than the boys in their hole in the ground. Just a chance the house might be scrubbed?"

Lucy ran to him and gave him such a hug that it nearly knocked him over. A clubhouse! And a stone one. It might be as good as anything in Canada. Then who could call Wales a rough wicked little town?

A Baby Dies
and a Baby Is Born

Very early next morning, while there was still a northern chill in the clear air, Father and Amory left to pick up the insurance adjuster at the dingy hotel on Main Street and then to drive off for the day. The Owens were also leaving early for a weekend of Bible classes in Hannah, Mr. Owen's other parish. So Lucy knew she would have a quiet day with Mother, something that hadn't happened often lately.

Mother already had plans. "I'm going to weed before it gets too hot, Lucy. Why don't you keep me company and do your week's stint of weeding so you'll have your other days free?"

"All right," agreed Lucy, "but be sure Father doesn't get mixed up later in the week. You know how Amory can raise a big fuss and say he's overworked and I'm spoiled, and then Father begins to think Amory's right."

"For goodness sakes, Lucy, who's raising the big fuss now?" Mother laughed as she took her big straw hat off the nail in the shed and handed Lucy's smaller one down to her. "Come on, let's get started," Mother said as she picked up the hoe beside the back door and led the way to the long rows of lettuce and radishes and onions.

Lucy chose to weed the lettuce row first, and after a few feet of weeding, she picked a tiny fresh green leaf and nibbled. It tasted both sweet and sharp, more like spring than hot summer.

Neither of them had finished even one row when they heard someone screaming, "Mrs. Johnston! Mrs. Johnston! The doctor! Quick!" And around the house came Hilda Dickerman, panting and yelling. "We got no phone. And Karlie's dying!"

Hilda rushed toward Mother. "Hurry! Hurry! It's poison!" She drew in a long hoarse breath. "And Ma wants me to get the priest and I don't know—"

Before Hilda finished, Mother dropped the hoe, picked up her long skirts and ran for the house faster than Lucy had ever seen her move. Hilda was at Mother's heels, and Lucy was close behind them.

By the time Lucy was indoors, Mother was already in the dining room, cranking the little black handle on the wall telephone and holding the oblong receiver to her ear. Nothing happened. So she cranked again as hard as she could, listened again, and shouted, "Hello? Hello?" But Lucy could tell that nobody was answering. Once more Mother cranked violently. Once more nothing happened.

Quickly Mother left the phone. "Nobody at the switchboard," she said. "Lucy, you run for Dr. Carmer.

Hilda, you run with Lucy, and she'll show you where Father Bronowski lives. And I'll go right over to your place, Hilda." And Mother ran out the front door and through the gate to the road, looking back only once to see that the girls were on their way.

Running down the back walk with Lucy, Hilda at first said nothing. Then by the time they had gone a block and were loping along past the Methodist church, Hilda said, "I was asleep, and Ma must have forgot to watch Karlie." Together the girls raced along another block of wooden sidewalks to the school corner. Then Hilda added, "I found him in the backyard with an old brown bottle, and it had—" she caught her breath, "it had that skull and bones sign on it."

She ran a few yards more, Lucy close beside her. "And now he's got like terrible fits. He mostly can't even breathe!" Hilda said no more.

Side by side the two girls ran along the rest of that block to Father Bronowski's house beside the Catholic church. "You knock there," Lucy pointed to the priest's big square house. "He might be over at the church for early mass, but you tell him how bad Karlie is, and he'll come. I know he will." And Lucy turned on to Main Street.

The first building on the street was the doctor's office and home. Lucy jerked open the screen door and pounded on the front door. The place looked deserted, its green shades all pulled down, but that might be because of the heat the day before. Lucy listened for someone coming to the door, but no one came.

Again she banged as hard as she could, listened again. Could it be that no one was home! The next time she not only banged on the door, but shouted, "Dr. Carmer! Dr. Carmer! A baby's dying. Come quick!"

This time Lucy did hear footsteps inside the house. In a moment the door opened a crack, but it was Mrs. Carmer who stood there and not the doctor.

"Oh, Mrs. Carmer, there's been a terrible accident and Karlie's dying and the doctor's got to come quick!" Lucy spilled it all out in one spasm.

Mrs. Carmer only opened the door a trifle wider and stood calmly inside the doorway. When she did speak, it was with a very quiet voice. "Lucy, you'll have to go back and say the doctor can't help anyone today. He's sick himself." And by the way Mrs. Carmer said *sick*, Lucy knew exactly what was wrong. Dr. Carmer, the only doctor for twenty miles around, was drunk.

"But the baby's dying—right now!" Lucy said, looking up at the tall quiet woman. "Does the doctor have any medicine to cure poison? Or does the drugstore have—" Then Lucy remembered. The village had no drugstore since last winter's fire. So she repeated what she'd said before. "He's a baby, and he's dying, Mrs. Carmer. I can't go back with nobody!"

Mrs. Carmer said only three words more. "I'm sorry, Lucy." Then the door was closed, and Lucy heard the inside lock snap shut also. It flashed through her mind that Mr. Owen was right. Wales was a wicked little town.

Lucy let the screen door shut by itself. In her mind she was asking, "Who else can you get when there's no doctor?" Then she remembered that Stan Sanderson had said his mother was home from a case in the country. Though Mrs. Sanderson was not a trained nurse, everybody said she was even better because she was a "born" nurse. She'd help. Lucy knew she would.

From the doctor's house to the Sandersons', the shortest way was behind the livery stable, but that was a path Lucy was forbidden to use. It went right past the blind pig, and even Amory had orders to stay off that path. But surely this time?

Almost before she knew it, Lucy had ducked behind the livery stable and was running in front of the unpainted one-room blind pig. She noticed its two dusty windows and its cracked door, but she was past it in a moment. Ahead of her was the Sandersons' bright green house, across the next street.

Lucy ran on, wearily now, but she could already see Mrs. Sanderson on the front stoop. As Lucy came through the gate, Mrs. Sanderson called to her, "Come and tell me all the news. I've been in the country for ten days. House is a mess, of course." Then she saw Lucy's expression. Before Lucy could say a word, Mrs. Sanderson stood up and hurried down the steps. "What's happened, Lucy? What's the trouble?" she asked.

"Come quick, Mrs. Sanderson. The doctor's drunk, and Karlie's dying!" Lucy forgot to explain who Karlie was, but who he was didn't make any difference to Mrs. Sanderson. In a matter of seconds, she untied her striped apron, reached inside the door for a little leather satchel, and returned to hurry out the gate with Lucy.

"Tell me where to go—no, I mean take me there," she said. Though Mrs. Sanderson was widely built like her son Stan, she had an efficient, determined step, and Lucy had to stretch her legs to keep up.

"It's Karlie Dickerman. They just moved into the Scott house," Lucy explained. "He's only two and he's beautiful and he ate poison from an old bottle because his mother's not able to watch him. She's sick." And as Lucy said that, she remembered another fact Father had told them the day before. "She's going to have another one," she added. "That must be what's wrong with her."

At this, Mrs. Sanderson, who specialized in births of babies, asked, "How soon?"

"How soon what?" Lucy wasn't sure of anything about the Dickermans beyond Hilda and Karlie. "Oh, you mean how soon will the baby come? I don't know. Nobody said."

They were now at the Dickermans' front gate, and Lucy could hear loud moans and a man's voice saying something very fast and low, like the priest's prayers that she had heard when Mother sometimes played the organ for a mass and took Lucy along with her.

Mother wasn't in sight, nor were Hilda or Father Bronowski. So Lucy stayed outside the gate while Mrs. Sanderson hurried into the house. In a moment Mother came out, the tears running down her cheeks from under her glasses. She caught Lucy tightly in her arms. Then she held her at a little distance and said, "You go on home, dear. I can't leave yet."

"And Karlie?" Lucy asked. But she knew the answer before she heard Mother say it.

"He died a few moments ago. I know, my dear, I know. Dr. Carmer couldn't come, could he?" And when Lucy was too choked to speak, Mother said, "Nothing could have saved Karlie. Don't blame the doctor or anyone. It just happened that way—that's all." Mother softly brushed back Lucy's hair from her forehead and kissed her.

Mother took off her glasses, wiped her eyes dry, and kept her lips tight shut for a second to stop their quivering. Then she straightened herself up and spoke firmly. "There's enough to weep about in there. You go on home and *do* something. If it's too hot to weed, pick up your room and dust the living room. At noon I'll come home, and we'll have dinner together."

As she started to go back into the house, Mother came to the gate again. "I should tell you, Lucy, that Mrs. Dickerman is very sick now, too. Probably the new baby will come today, and if it does—" Mother paused, "well, it will be a seven-month baby, so there's no telling. It's touch and go."

For Lucy's comfort, Mother now said, "It's lucky you brought Stan's mother. If anyone can save Hilda's mother and such a tiny baby, it's Mrs. Sanderson." With that, Mother disappeared into the house, where the mass-talk had ceased but the moans never stopped.

The rest of the morning was endless. Lucy puttered about the house, trying to think of something besides the Dickermans, but that, of course, was impossible. She finally took Topsy out in the yard and put her through her routine of tricks—sitting up to beg, waltzing a few steps on her hind legs, and lying down to play dead.

But at her own command, "Topsy, play dead!" Lucy burst into tears and ran back into the house. Topsy followed, and when Lucy lay on the sofa crying big tears, Topsy jumped up and tried to lick her face. She hugged Topsy close and murmured, "Topsy, my Topsy, don't you die!"

At noon, Mother came home, looking very tired. In spite of the day being cooler than yesterday, Mother did not suggest the usual hot dinner. Instead they ate sandwiches of jelly and peanut butter and drank big glasses of milk as they sat on the wooden porch swing that hung by chains from the porch ceiling.

When they were done, Mother went upstairs to bathe and change and she came down ready to give her two lessons.

"Mother, you aren't going to give music lessons today, are you?" Lucy was shocked.

"If there were anything I could do now at the Dickermans', I'd do it," Mother said. "But the baby isn't born yet, and Mrs. Sanderson is there, and Father Bronowski has promised to meet the train to tell Mr. Dickerman what has happened. So I'd only be in the way."

Lucy must still have looked uncertain, for Mother went on. "The Schmidts drive a long way to town for me to give the girls their lessons, and I'm sure they've already started. What good would it do anyone for me to say that I can't teach today?"

It made sense. Lucy could see that. But Mother was such a softhearted woman, how could she put Karlie out of her mind and listen to scales and finger exercises? Later, while the lessons were going on, Lucy sat under the cottonwoods, holding Topsy on her lap and trying to read her July *Saint Nicholas* magazine.

But the story of two rival princes or the one about a girls' boarding school didn't interest her. What kept coming back to her was what Gwin had repeated yesterday, right here under the trees: "Wales is a rough wicked little town, and no one cares for the children."

Could that be true? Was Karlie dead because no one cared for him? But they did care. Hilda loved him. You could see she did. Yet he had slipped out of the house and swallowed poison and died.

Then from the open windows came the sound of Mother's music, as she played a few bars of a new piece to show Mattie Schmidt how it should go. Lucy felt as though the music was mourning for Karlie, and for the Dickermans, and for all the children who grew up in rough wicked little Wales. And again, she cried.

Late in the afternoon Mother went back to the Dickermans' and soon returned to say, "Lucy, such good news. There's a baby boy, and he's very, very small. But Mrs. Sanderson says that he's stronger than many she's seen at seven months."

"Mother, I have to ask," Lucy queried. "I've never seen a seven-month baby. He's not really finished, is he?" And then she thought of Karlie. "Will the new boy ever be as beautiful as Karlie, do you think?"

"Who knows?" Mother answered. "Anyway, he's going to live, and that's because you got Mrs. Sanderson there. For a few days she'll care for him and for Mrs. Dickerman, while Hilda looks after the rest of them and keeps house."

Shortly before suppertime, Father and Amory drove up. Mother and Lucy both went out to open and close the big gate. Before Amory was out of the Regal, he was boasting of his scores in hitting knotholes in fenceposts. But he'd barely begun, when Mother said, "Shhhh, Amory. I want to tell you both something."

And Mother told them of the death of Karlie and the birth of the tiny new baby. Even Amory, who had never seen Karlie, had tears in his eyes. Father shook his head sadly as he repeated, "Those poor Dickermans."

As they went into the house together, Father said in his serious deep voice, "I won't go over tonight, Caroline, but when you go, tell Pete he can count on me for whatever he may need."

"I'll be going over to spell Mrs. Sanderson later on," Mother said. "I'll tell him. I know what you mean. They'll need cash, won't they?"

For the second time that day Lucy was surprised by Mother. First the music lessons and now talk of cash when a baby had just died. But this time Lucy said nothing. She understood that a funeral, a sick mother, a sickly baby and Mrs. Sanderson's nursing would all cost money.

Because it would be light until nearly ten o'clock, Father gave Amory permission to find Jerry and Stan and report on his target shooting. Then Father and Lucy, left alone, sat on the porch swing, and together they slowly swung to and fro in the shade of the vines.

"Father, can you tell me why—" Lucy began.

But Father may have guessed she was going to ask questions about Karlie's death, so he immediately began a teaching session. "Lucy, I wish you'd been with us today. In the reeds by Rush Lake we saw four baby mud hens. I've never seen any so tiny."

Lucy started over. "Father, about Karlie and about Wales—do you think—"

Father again tried to sidetrack her. "And in a very damp spot near the mud hens, I found a single moccasin flower. Some bird must have carried the seed from a woodsy place," he said. "Remember all the facts I taught you about the way seeds can spread?"

Sometimes Father was too much the professor he once had been, and Lucy knew his lecture might go on and on.

"Father, you've got to stop and listen to me." She spoke almost sharply. "I want to ask you something. I want to know why Karlie had to die." Having gone this far, she went on to ask about the doctor too. "And why did Dr. Carmer have to be drunk just when he should have been a doctor? Whose fault is all this?" She sat watching his face, waiting for an answer.

"If I knew the answers to those questions, Lucy, I'd be the wisest man in the world," Father answered. Then he added exactly what Mother had said earlier. "Don't try to blame anyone, Lucy. Some things—some very sad things—just happen, that's all."

"You don't think it's because of Wales, do you,

Father?" Lucy wanted to tell him what Mr. Owen had said but decided she had better not. So she spoke as though they were her own words. "Do you think it happened because Wales is a rough wicked town?"

"What made you think such a thing?" Father asked. "Wales is no different from villages everywhere. Blaming Wales—what a silly idea!" Then he abruptly shifted. "Now let's talk about fixing up your playhouse."

"Playhouse! Father, it's a clubhouse!" and Lucy was so provoked that she did begin to talk about the stone house.

The Raid
on the Blind Pig

There won't be an Owen around until tomorrow, Lucy," Father said after Sunday breakfast. "Why not come with me?"

"Depends on where you're going," Lucy answered.

"I have to catch up on work at the bank, but first I'm taking some papers to Mrs. Bortz for her to sign. Come on along. She always likes to see you, and you could see the inside of her new house."

"Oh, do go, Lucy," said Mother. "Guinevere's finished that last volume of the Dotty Dimple series, and Mrs. Bortz wants to read it."

"I'll take it, but I don't see why an old woman wants to borrow those Dotty Dimples. They're for first graders," Lucy said, scornfully.

"But Mrs. Bortz grew up in Germany a long time ago,

and English is hard for her," Mother reminded Lucy.

"You come, and I'll tell you another reason. It's almost a secret," Father said, as he shoved a thick envelope of papers into his coat pocket. Lucy tucked the little blue book under her arm.

As they went through the backyard together, Father talked, but not about Mrs. Bortz. "Wales is only a village, Lucy, but if you knew half of what I know about the lives of people here, you'd know a lot about the rest of the world."

Oh, dear, thought Lucy. One of Father's lectures.

"There's old Mrs. Bortz, for instance. You might not believe it, but she grew up in a very rich family in Germany. She lived in a big house—you could call it a mansion—with more servants than in Dotty Dimple's house. Do you know what I think?" Father looked down at Lucy, and waited for her to answer.

"Well, go on. What do you think?" asked Lucy.

"I think she reads those stories because they remind her of her childhood, even if Dotty Dimple lived in a big house in Portland, Maine, and Mrs. Bortz lived in a big house in Germany."

"But why didn't she stay where she was rich?" To Lucy, all this sounded more like a magazine story than like Wales.

"You're a favorite of hers, you know, so I don't think she'd mind if I told you. She says she always wanted a girl—had those five sons instead. And when Mr. Bortz died last year and I was executor of his will—all those wills I see—"

"I know, I know," Lucy interrupted. "What's the rest of her story? We're almost there."

"She eloped. That's her story. Adam Bortz was a young farmer and must have been very handsome. And she found life dull and boring in the big house." Father was talking faster now, trying to pack everything into these last few steps to her yard.

"He was going to America, so she had him buy a ticket for her, too. Then she simply walked out of her father's house, caught the train going to the seaport, and married Adam the day before they sailed."

"And she came to Wales? To a homestead?" Lucy couldn't imagine it.

"Yes, to Wales, North Dakota, and Adam did well, and they had those five handsome sons."

"And was she beautiful, too, Father, when you first came to Wales, before I was born?" Lucy asked.

"Not storybook beautiful, Lucy. She'd already had those five children, and she'd worked hard, in the garden and the barn as well as in the house. All the farm women did that. She was already old and tired when we met her," Father said. "But when we go in now, look at the good lines in her face. It's a face that hasn't turned sour or coarse."

After Father rapped hard a couple of times on the shiny varnished front door, Mrs. Bortz slowly opened it and then smiled broadly. Since it was nearly time for mass, she had on her best black dress and her black hat with black flowers and a black veil. But the black was not at all forbidding. For her at the end of a long life, black seemed right.

"Mr. Johnston! Come in, and my Lucy, too. Come in, come in," and Mrs. Bortz led them into her small square living room. There were four straight chairs around a table, her own high wooden rocker, and a tall chest of drawers with photos on it.

"Just look," she said as she lifted down two photos. "Now Adam's dead, my little sister sends me pictures of her two boys, and she says to me, 'Come home,' and I say, 'Go home? Wales is my home now.' " And she began to talk in German with Father, while Lucy looked at the two small photos.

They weren't pictures of boys, of course. They were grown men in soldier's uniforms, German uniforms and not ordinary ones, Lucy was sure of that. Extra buttons and loops of braid were all across their jackets.

As Lucy stared at the men in their high-collared jackets, Mrs. Bortz began to speak in English again. "Officers they are, Lucy. Officers in their Kaiser's army. *Ach*, may God watch over them and bring them safe home to their mother. And such fine men she says they are. And both so good to her, so good."

Lucy was startled. These were Huns? What the Owens called The Enemy? How could Huns be good to their mothers? Surely that couldn't be, not after all she'd heard about their shooting old women and little children.

The papers were now signed, and Lucy handed over the Dotty Dimple book that she'd nearly forgotten. "Mother sent you this, Mrs. Bortz. She remembered it was the one Dotty Dimple that you hadn't read," Lucy explained.

"After mass, I begin it—I do," grinned Mrs. Bortz. "The print's easy and the English—easy too." Then to Father she said, "Never time to learn good English—always too much to do, too much to do."

They walked with her across the street to the door of the Catholic church. Afterward, on the way along Main Street, Father at first was silent. Then he began to talk, very seriously.

"There's no way to tell you, Lucy," he said, "how hard it was for me when I first came here to run the bank. The only German I knew was university German, and every single German farmer spoke a German dialect. I couldn't do business with a blessed one of them, and I thought I'd have to give up. But guess who saved me?" He didn't wait for Lucy to guess. "Mrs. Bortz saved me. Of course she spoke my proper German, and she tutored me in the bad German. It saved my job—and saved me, too, I think."

Then at the door of the bank, he joked, "Now Lucy, I've got to count the millions and juggle silver and weigh the gold." He gave her a pat on the head to start her home, unlocked the bank door, and went in.

Lucy turned toward home. The sun was already blistering hot, and she was tempted to cut behind the livery stable, in the shade of the buildings. Nobody would know. On all Main Street there was no one, not even in the wooden chairs in front of the livery stable. She saw one empty auto and that was all. She had used the shortcut the day before, and it certainly was cooler. She'd chance it, she decided, though it was against every family rule.

So she slipped between the stable and the butcher shop, quickening her steps because she knew she was where she shouldn't be. In no time she was out of sight of Main Street and in front of the blind pig. Looking up, she saw three husky men standing by the closed door, all three strangers to her, and all as amazed to see her as she was to see them.

Then one man turned directly toward her, and on his jacket she saw the shiny sheriff's badge. She began to sprint, but not before she heard one man yell, "Open up, in the name of the Law!" and another man shout, "Come on out! You're under arrest!"

The door must have opened and someone must have come out, but she wouldn't have looked back for 100

dollars—not for 1,000! All the rest of the way home she raced at top speed, feeling as though the Law was after her too. And as she ran, she made up her mind that she wouldn't say a word about it to anyone. It would only get her into trouble. After all, she wasn't supposed to go on that path, ever.

When she came to her own block, Lucy slowed to a jog trot. At the little house next to her own back gate, she was surprised to see old Mrs. Schnitzler weeding in her crowded front garden. Mrs. Schnitzler, who went to mass every single morning of her life, at home weeding during Sunday church? What could have happened? Lucy couldn't be nosy and ask, but Mrs. Schnitzler was ready to talk without being asked. She waddled over to the fence and spoke.

"Lucy, your pa—he's home today?" she asked.

"He'll soon be coming home for Sunday dinner, Mrs. Schnitzler," Lucy paused to answer. "You'll see him."

"Yah, I'll vatch. I vant to ask him. That Pole, Father Bronowski—yesterday in mass—he vent—that baby—I think he sin," and Mrs. Schnitzler gave up in English and switched to German. So in a chink of silence, Lucy waved and hurried through her own gate, wondering who had sinned. Surely not little Karlie and surely not the priest either. A priest couldn't sin—or could he in a wicked village like Wales?

At dinnertime, Father came in, hopping mad about something. At the table he said, "Caroline, I never saw such people for worrying about the wrong things! Mrs. Schnitzler says—" And that was as far as Father went, for Amory came bursting in.

"Guess what Jerry saw this morning. He was late for mass, and he was running like a steam engine along Main Street and around behind the livery stable, you know, at the blind pig, he heard a yell like this—" Amory took a fresh lungful of air and bellowed— " 'Open up! In the name of the Law!' " So Jerry snuck behind the livery stable and peeked.

"And do you know what he saw? Three men he'd never seen before, and he thinks the bulges on their hips were revolvers—could have been. Then another man yelled, 'Open up!' and the door opened and one man came out—just one. Jerry watched them hustle that one man into their auto and drive off like lightning—maybe twenty-five or even thirty miles an hour, Jerry guessed." Amory's excitement changed for a moment to disappointment. "Golly, a raid in Wales, and I missed it!"

"Strange time for a raid, Sunday morning," Father said. "I'm surprised there was anyone there at all." Then he spoke to Mother. "Sure enough, someone was tipped off in advance. Trying to close that blind pig hasn't ever done any good—too many people in cahoots. Did Jerry see who was the one man arrested, Amory?" Father asked.

"Sure he did. Jerry was close as anything. He says he could see the bullets in the—well, he could have seen the bullets if he could have seen the revolvers, he was that close to—"

"But who was arrested, Amory? Who was that one man?"

"It was a Morgan, all right, Luke Morgan, that Canadian cousin of theirs," Amory answered. "The one we left the magazines for yesterday."

"Those skunks!" Father was really angry. "The old man must have sent Luke to town on an errand when he knew there was going to be a raid."

"Will he go to the penitentiary?" Mother asked. "You said he's of age now. Or will being a Canadian make a difference, Harry?" Mother sounded as worried as if Luke were her own son in trouble.

"I'll find out what I can," Father said. "But my guess is that the sheriff needs a prisoner to show for the raid. A raid with nobody caught would make him look silly. So it might go hard with Luke. Anyway, I can't do anything for him until his case comes up in court."

Mother looked down at the table. "Here's this nice chicken dinner and nobody enjoying it."

A knock at the back door made Amory jump up, sure that it was Stan. After a few moments Amory was back at the table. Stan had gone to the cave to wait until dinner was over.

"Wow! Stan says it was somebody right here in Wales that sent word to the sheriff to make a raid—just as though that blind pig was something new. And Stan says everybody in town is trying to find out who did such a—"

Amory could go on forever, so Mother interrupted. "Lucy, help me clear the dinner plates and bring in the lemon pie."

Lucy was glad to leave the table, for this once she knew more than Amory. But it wouldn't do any good to tattle on Mr. Owen anyway.

As she ate her pie, she was thinking of what Mr. Owen had done to Luke Morgan. "Who's wicked now?" she asked herself. "Mr. Owen is teaching the Bible up in Hannah today, and he doesn't even know what he's done to Luke, the only good Morgan and a Canadian, too."

Amory gulped his pie and hurried out to the cave. This time he didn't beg for pie to take with him, though Lucy thought a lemon pie would plaster anyone who fell in better than a rhubarb one.

After Amory had banged his way out the back door, Mother asked, "Harry before all this blind pig business, you started to say something about Mrs. Schnitzler. What was it?"

"Well, when Karlie Dickerman was dying," Father began, "Father Bronowski rushed off before the mass was done. And the old women who go to mass every morning think he committed a sin not to finish the mass first. So none of them went to mass at all today. What do you think of that?" Father was very red in the face and angry again.

"Doesn't it count that a baby was dying? Is it really a sin for a priest to break off the mass?" Mother sounded as puzzled as Lucy had been.

"I know enough about the mass to straighten out Mrs. Schnitzler." Father brightened for a moment. "Now the poor old soul thinks she sinned because she stayed home from mass today."

"Tell us, King Solomon," Mother teased, "how did you judge the priest?"

"Oh, he had finished all but the last words, and those aren't necessary, even though she's used to hearing them at the end. The real trouble, Caroline, is that the Germans don't like Father Bronowski because he's a Pole. But he's a good priest, and here they call him wicked because he runs to a dying baby." And Father let out a loud "Huh!"

"Wicked, indeed!" Mother exclaimed. "Some people have no idea of what's really wicked in this village!"

And what is really wicked in Wales? Lucy wondered. But Father had been so cross when she asked him about Wales that she wasn't going to try asking Mother.

The Cave Men and the Stone Age Girls

The next morning Mother spent a few minutes at the Dickermans', but she returned home, reporting that so many friends and relatives were there that they didn't need one more person to crowd that small cottage.

"And the new baby boy, Mother?" Lucy asked.

"I saw him this morning, or rather I saw the cardboard box lined with cotton batting. The top of his head showed, and a very tiny head, I must say," replied Mother.

"Did you see Hilda?" Lucy continued.

"No, Hilda took the twins over to the Kinsers' so her mother could have a little quiet. But with all those folks talking, it's not very quiet." Mother shook her head and looked out the kitchen window, speaking almost to herself. "If I'd lost one baby and just had a new one, I'd not want—" then she stopped.

"Well, here come Gwendolyn, Gwinyth and Guinevere. Tell them right away about the stone house," Mother said cheerfully.

Lucy saw that Mother wanted her to think of something happier than Karlie's death, but once the girls had settled on their old blanket under the cottonwoods, Lucy began talking about it.

Lucy wanted the girls to feel as sad as she did about Karlie, so she started to tell the story as though it were one from a book. But suddenly it wasn't a story in a book. She saw Karlie running out the back door in his undershirt, laughing and grabbing cookies. And she burst into tears. With her sobs and the catches in her breath, she couldn't go on. She didn't have a handkerchief, and no one else had one either.

So she ran weeping into the house. There Mother produced a handkerchief, and she also asked, "You do want the Owens here today, don't you, Lucy?" And when Lucy assured her that she did, Mother said, "I've been thinking that the sooner you girls move into the stone house, the better. I'll pay everybody five cents apiece—girls and boys—to clean out the coal dust right away."

"Oh, Mother, how absolutely terrific!" and Lucy rushed out the front door, her tears only half-mopped. Waving Mother's handkerchief, she called to the girls.

"What I haven't told you is that we four girls can have the stone house for a clubhouse, and now Mother's decided to pay everybody a nickel apiece for cleaning it today—beginning right now!" For a moment Lucy saw a surprised expression on the girls' faces. So swift a change in her spirits seemed wrong to Lucy, too, but she couldn't help it.

"As soon as Mother finishes some baking, she's coming to start us off. She won't be long. But I wonder," Lucy said, as she looked at their clean dresses, "shouldn't you go home first and put on something awfully old?"

"We'll be back in ten minutes," said Gwen, and she and Guinnie set off in a run for home. Gwin stayed behind, to give Topsy another pat, but also to satisfy her curiosity.

"Lucy, were both the priest and the doctor drunk?" Gwin asked as she stood up.

"Not both," Lucy began slowly, for she could see that she must speak carefully or Mr. Owen would have more proof of the wickedness of Wales. "Dr. Carmer must have had too much to drink, but he's going away pretty soon to take the Cure." Since Lucy had no idea what the Cure was, she hurried on.

"And Father Bronowski stopped his mass and ran as fast as he could with Hilda. And he got there in time, and he's been so good to all of them that Mother says—"

"I just wondered," Gwin interrupted. "Nothing like this ever happened where we lived before. Imagine, finding poison in your own backyard!" And Gwin went off toward the parsonage.

"She makes it sound as though we grow poison in our gardens," Lucy said to herself, as she rolled Topsy into one corner of the blanket and carried her into the house.

Mother was now out by the cave, asking Amory and Stan and Jerry if they wanted to come up and help clean the stone house for five cents each. Quickly the three boys—one after the other—emerged from their pit.

Mother began giving orders. "Lucy, get the two old cellar brooms and my scrubbing brush from the shed. Jerry, you fill the two pails I put beside the pump. Amory and Stan, you pull the ladder up from the cave so we can lean it against the house and clean those two small end windows." Then just as they all started to obey orders, she said, "Wait! First, help me cover this cave so it's shut tight for an hour or two."

Soon the Owen girls were back in old clothes, but they had the spotless Edward with them. His short pants were light tan, and his shirt was pure white. Five minutes in the coal house, and Edward would be a disaster. Fortunately Lucy remembered that Amory's old overalls and a torn blue shirt were hanging in the shed.

"Mother, couldn't we put Edward into old clothes just until the coal dust settles?" Lucy asked.

"Why not? That way he can have a good time," Mother said.

So Lucy and Guinnie took Edward indoors to change. Once he was stripped of his fancy suit and buttoned into Amory's faded blue shirt and farm-boy overalls, he looked like a new boy.

"Edward, you've grown in just the little while you've lived in Wales, haven't you? And you're more grown up—not just taller," Lucy said to encourage him. "You'll soon be a Cave Man." But Edward didn't need encouraging. He was delighted with the shirt's torn elbows, and he admired the brass buckles that fastened the overall straps at the shoulders.

"I like them so much," he announced, "I don't want ever to wear anything else. I'll keep 'em," and he swaggered a little, trying to be a farm boy.

"Of course, you can wear them whenever you like," Lucy said. "And you really need them when you work."

As they all scrubbed and washed and swept the little house, Mother stayed nearby to oversee the job. She gave everyone a turn swishing on the pails of well water, and she insisted that Amory stop bossing and do his share. The boys climbed up the ladder to clean the two windows, the girls washed the door, and everyone brushed the stone walls, inside and out.

"Hey, Mother," Amory finally suggested, "how about us three boys climbing up on the old wooden roof and stomping a little—just to be sure it's strong?" He began to climb the ladder, but at that moment Mother passed out the nickels, and the Cave Men raced toward the village for their ice-cream cones.

The girls and Edward paused to think how their money should be spent. Guinnie and Edward decided on cones, but they'd have to wait until the older girls took them to Main Street later. Gwen, Gwin and Lucy had other ideas.

"Perhaps if we have a club, we should have a treasury," said Lucy.

"Of course," Gwen said. "We'll have a treasurer and a president and vice-president and secretary. Isn't it lucky that there are four of us, everybody an officer."

"How about me?" Edward demanded. "The Cave Men won't have me, and I'm not a girl for your club, so what am I?"

To Lucy, he had always seemed like a spoiled brat, but in his ragged overalls he didn't look nearly so bratty. Yet the only man for a girls' clubhouse would be a janitor. So she said brightly, "Edward, you can be our janitor."

Edward let out a yell, Guinnie looked hurt, and both Gwen and Gwin spoke at once. "Lucy, how awful! Edward Albert Christian Owen a janitor?"

I suppose it's Canada again that I don't understand, thought Lucy. Aloud she said, "I was only wondering."

Mother then came back, and hearing of the problem of Edward, she suggested, "Why not have Edward be the club mascot?" Edward looked uncertain. "You know a mascot doesn't ever have to work," Mother explained, "and a mascot is always different from the regular members."

"That would do it," Lucy agreed. "A mascot like the tiger Father says one college has, and another has a bulldog."

Gwen now spoke to Mother very politely but very definitely. "Mrs. Johnston, I don't think Mama and Papa would like Edward being a bulldog. Couldn't he be a squire, like the junior knights that I've read about?"

They all felt that was perfect for Edward—very aristocratic, almost royal, and certainly suitable for a boy named for the future king of England.

"Now that Edward's settled, let's plan your furnishings," said Mother. So they all stepped into the freshly scrubbed stone house and discussed what they might use. Lucy had a small table, two straight chairs to match, and two rockers. Mother had a pair of rag rugs, and the Owens had wooden boxes for shelves and cupboards.

"And curtains, what for curtains?" asked Gwen.

Mother looked up at the two tiny windows. "I must have something—let me see—"

Gwin interrupted. "I do wish we had chintz. All the nicest living rooms in Canada had chintz."

"Had what?" asked Lucy. Canada was only a few miles across the prairie from Wales, but that Canada was Manitoba. Eastern Canada, which the Owens came from, had been settled much longer and was more like England. So to Lucy, everything about their Canada was remarkable, and chintz sounded very remarkable.

"Oh, you know—chintz! I do wish we had chintz," repeated Gwin.

Lucy looked around, and for the first time she noticed

that the Owens—except for Gwin—didn't have much chin. But surely she couldn't have heard right—*chins* for window curtains?

Mother answered Gwin before Lucy could ask again. "The cloth I have isn't shiny like chintz, Gwin, but I do have some with bright flowers on it—and I believe it's just enough."

"That sounds perfect," said Gwen, who always wanted everyone to be happy. And they all trooped in and out of the house, carrying their furnishings.

Before long, the Cave Men were back, their cones in their stomachs. They hauled away the ladder, uncovered the cave, and disappeared into its depths.

Gwin sat rocking in one of the little chairs, looking out their door toward the cave. "Why don't we put up our own sign?" she asked. "They've still got that NO WO MEN ALL OWED. What will ours say? Where's a shingle?"

Edward found a small shingle, Guinnie lent a black crayon, and they all worked on the words. Finally, the sign was stuck in the ground in front of their house. It read:

NO   EN

TRANCE

FOR   BOYS

Of course, the next time that Amory came to the surface, he read the sign. "Boys! Don't call us boys! We're Cave Men! Can't you even read? What a bunch of dummies!" he yelled.

"We've got a stone house, and you've only got a hole in the ground," yelled Lucy. "You're no better than gophers!"

"You girls are just playing house in a playhouse,"

taunted Stan, as he also came out of the cave.

"It's made of stone, and you can't hurt it!" screamed Edward, who was feeling his importance as a squire in overalls.

"We can too!" shouted Amory, and, lifting a stone from the heap of dirt beside the cave, he heaved it toward the clubhouse. Of course it didn't hit the house. Amory had sense enough not to let it.

"Yeah, we're Cave Men!" he yelled. "You're just Stone Age girls! And Cave Men always beat up Stone Age girls!"

By that time Jerry was out, too, and they were all shouting. And the four girls and Edward began screaming and screeching to drown out the Cave Men's insults.

Mother came out just in time to see Amory leading a full-scale attack on the girls' house. Her own yell added to the general uproar. "Amory, what on earth are you doing now?"

Everyone stopped screaming, and the three boys scrambled back toward their cave. Amory began to explain. "Well, Mother, we think if they live in a stone house that they must be Stone Age girls. And we're Cave Men, and so—well, you've read about prehistoric times, haven't you, Mother?

"Indeed I have," Mother scolded, "and there will be no prehistoric times in my backyard! You Cave Men go down in your cave, and you girls finish settling your house. Later on I'll bring out food for all of you."

"Food!" shouted Amory. "Cave Men like it raw and lots of it. Sissy Stone Age girls like it cooked. They're too civilized for us!"

The Cave Men climbed down into their cave. Mother went back to her kitchen. And the girls entered their stone house, that so far hadn't been a very safe hideout.

The Circus Truce

Inside their clubhouse, the girls began a meeting. "First a club name," Gwin said. "We'll be here every morning before those lazy boys, so how about Early Birds?"

"I vote against that," said Gwen. "You know what the early birds get—worms! Not my favorite dish."

"How about Sunshine Helpers?" asked Guinnie. At this, the older girls all shouted, "Never!" Guinnie looked downcast, so Gwen had to comfort her.

"It's nice when Mother calls you that, Guinnie, but a club of Sunshine Helpers sounds like a bunch of house-cleaners."

"Couldn't we be the Stone House Club? That sounds good, and we'll always meet here," Gwin suggested.

"That won't work," Lucy said rather unhappily. "You girls don't have an older brother, but I can tell you, Amory and the Cave Men have called us the Stone Age Girls—and we're stuck with that name."

"The Stone Age Girls—sounds fierce and powerful. And it does fit the house, I suppose," Gwen said, accepting the name. So they went on to choose officers. As the oldest, Gwen had to be president. And since Gwin had trouble adding two and two and coming out with the right answer, she was made vice-president, and Lucy agreed to be treasurer and to help Guinnie's spelling as secretary.

But Edward, the squire—what on earth could Edward do? Gwen settled that problem. "Perhaps we don't have to decide that," she said. "Edward's not much of a doer. Can't he just be? Be a squire, I mean?"

Next they debated a motto. At first they liked "Cemented together," which was really how the stones made their house. "And we'll always be cemented in friendship, too," Lucy remarked.

"Cemented in friendship might be all right," Gwen said, "but doesn't it sound as though the four of us were stuck in concrete, like Siamese twins doubled?" Gwen began to giggle.

"But we've got to get stones into it, haven't we?" Lucy insisted, after they'd stopped giggling. So they began to think of mottoes that included stones, like "A rolling stone gathers no moss," which Gwin didn't like. "Who wants moss all over her anyway?"

Then Gwen suggested "People who live in glass houses shouldn't throw stones." But no one wanted a glass house competing with their stone one.

Finally they decided a motto should encourage you when you're ready to give up. So they chose "Leave no stone unturned."

"Now for the regalia," Gwen said.

"Re— what?" echoed Gwin, who was sometimes puzzled by the words Gwen and Lucy learned from books.

"Re-ga-li-a," repeated Gwen. "It's special costumes for when you're at club meetings."

"What did Stone Age girls wear?" asked Guinnie. "Shouldn't we dress the way they did?"

"Good heavens, no!" shrieked Lucy. "Why, Guinnie, they mostly didn't wear anything at all, sometimes just a little piece of animal skin or fur perhaps. Imagine, in winter when it's forty below zero and deep snow, having a meeting without a stitch on!" And they all went off into another fit of giggles.

Topsy, roused from her snooze on Lucy's lap, jumped down, shook herself and walked out of the clubhouse.

"Look, Topsy's afraid we'll use her fur coat for our regalia," shouted Gwin, and they began laughing so hard that they sounded like a whole tribe of girls.

Just then, Jerry came up from the cave with a pail of dirt. "What's the joke? Tell us too," he called.

But the girls thought that jokes about meetings with no clothes on were not right to tell the boys, so they stopped laughing and all moved outside, as Gwin yelled to Jerry, "Don't you wish you knew?"

Amory came up, followed by Stan, and the three Cave Men moved toward the stone house. The girls retreated inside.

In an instant, the three boys rushed to the stone house, slammed the door, and pushed the wooden peg through the metal hasp to lock it.

The girls began to howl. The boys yelled, "Yeah! Yeah! Yeah! Now we've got you! You're locked in, and we won't let you out all day!"

Once more Mother appeared. "Can't you leave the

girls alone?" At the sound of her yell, the girls stopped their shouting. "You boys stay in your hideout. That's what your cave is for!" Mother said as she pulled the peg out of the lock and opened the stone-house door.

"Now you boys—vamoose!" Mother ordered, using a slang word Lucy had never heard her use before. "And you girls come along with me. We'll sit under the cottonwoods while the Cave Men descend into their darkness. I've made coconut macaroons, and the boys can wait for theirs."

Mother first led the girls and Edward to the kitchen for two macaroons each, and then she went with them to sit in the shade a few minutes. "I'm exhausted," she said, "and it isn't even noon yet."

Right away, Gwin thanked Mother for the sulfur ointment. "Mrs. Johnston, it worked, and it worked on Papa's hands too. He was sure he had prickly heat, but of course it was prairie itch. And do you know what he said?"

Lucy braced herself for what Mr. Owen might have said. Mr. Owen with the itch? Lucy was horrified.

"Papa said," continued Gwin, "every day he's here he learns something new. He thinks people have to know a lot to live in villages like Wales."

Lucy was relieved that Mr. Owen was learning something, after all. She could almost forgive him for what he'd said earlier.

Before Mother could answer, Gwin began a new subject, while she slowly chewed on a macaroon. "Do you think, Mrs. Johnston, we could somehow make friends with the boys?"

Mother looked doubtful. "Gwinyth, I'm not sure that Cave Men are ever civilized enough to be friends with any girls, but there's one thing you can try. Can you think of anything you could all work on together?"

"Like our cleaning the stone house this morning?" asked Gwen.

"Yes, but we can't clean house everyday, can we? Besides, Mrs. Johnston would run out of nickels," said the practical Guinnie.

"I was wondering about a program you might all do together," Mother continued, thinking aloud.

"Oh, Mother, how about a circus!" exclaimed Lucy. The circus that she had missed still lingered in her mind. "We can all do something—Topsy can do tricks, and Amory has his magician's set, and Jerry can stand on his head, and Gwin can sing, and—"

"No," Gwin said, "I could be the hula dancer."

"Hula dancer!" Mother's eyes opened wide. "No hula dancers in this circus, Gwinyth. Where on earth did you hear of hula dancers?"

"Sometimes in Canada circuses have them, I've heard," Gwin said, looking down rather sheepishly.

"And what can Edward and I do?" asked Guinnie. "We don't have a trick dog, and we can't sing like Gwin, and we want to be in it too."

"Maybe Edward could be a clown?" Mother spoke hesitantly, for even she was not sure about a boy with three royal names.

"Oh, not a clown," Gwen answered hastily. "How about his salute to the Canadian flag? He does that beautifully."

"And if Gwin will sing the words, Edward and I can act our mushroom song," Guinnie said happily.

Mother looked unsure about the words of any song that Gwin might choose, but she nodded and went on to say, "You could do it on the sixth. That will give you a couple of days to get ready. You girls will have to make the costumes and set up boxes and chairs in the barn and keep the little children out of trouble. And I'll phone, asking mothers to come."

"I'll go ask the boys right away," said Gwin, jumping up to start for the cave.

"Not now!" Mother almost barked. "The Cave Men are at rest in their cave, and I must get a little housework done. When the boys come up for dinner, it will be soon enough. I'll get them to agree to a circus truce."

After the girls had gone home and Lucy was setting the dinner table, Mrs. Owen phoned Mother. Lucy could hear every word Mrs. Owen spoke, she was so upset. "Mrs. Johnston, I'm so sorry to trouble you, but our Edward came home without his clothes on."

Mother gave a little gasp, and Mrs. Owen corrected herself. "Oh, he had clothes on, but they certainly weren't his. Guinnie says his are over at your house, and I'll send her over for them right away, before his papa sees him in overalls." Mrs. Owen calmed down before she went on. "I do hope you understand, and I'm so sorry he took Amory's clothes. Guinnie'll bring them back."

"Of course, I understand," Mother answered. "The boys and girls had a—well, they had a disagreement in our backyard, and there was so much going on that I completely forgot Edward's suit. It's right here, all neatly folded on a chair."

Coming away from the phone, Mother said to Lucy, "Sometimes I wonder what that boy will grow up to be."

"Not a Cave Man, that's sure," said Lucy, laughing. "But some day, Mother, I would like to see chintz."

"When we go to Minneapolis, Lucy, you shall see chintz," promised Mother. "It's nothing marvelous. All that sewing Mrs. Owen does is better than dozens of bolts of chintz. She's the marvel, even if I don't agree with her about how to bring up a boy in a village like Wales."

At dinner that day, as Father was putting the first helping of meat pie on Mother's plate, the phone rang. Amory was up in a jiffy, standing on tiptoe with the receiver at his ear. "Hello!" he bellowed. "Langdon calling my father? He's right here."

Father took the receiver from Amory, and everyone strained to hear what came over the wire. They could hear only enough to know that the voice belonged to Father's brother, Uncle Charlie Johnston in Langdon. Father's answers told the rest.

"George, Ed, and Len all coming on the train this afternoon for over the Fourth?" Lucy felt excited immediately. Her cousins had been born in North Dakota, as she had, and she'd known them all her life, but still a visit from them was always something special.

Meantime Father was listening while Uncle Charlie's voice went on—a far-off rumble. Then Father said, "You're quite right. You and Effie should go off alone for those three days and let Gen stay with her friend. And of course you shouldn't take Ed with you."

More distant words. Finally, Father finished. "If Kink is all right alone, we'll expect the other three boys on the train today. Fine! The more boys the better for the Fourth of July." And he hung up.

Father came back to the table, rubbing his hands. "Three more boys to fall into your cave, Mrs. Johnston —and all good-sized ones!"

"It's not my cave. You know that very well," Mother protested. "But, Harry—Ed for the Fourth of July? Aren't the fireworks enough noise?"

Lucy understood. Her cousin George was a sober,

busy kind of boy, already in his teens. Len, not quite as old as Lucy, was the youngest and only now catching up to the others in size and energy and lungs. But Ed, slightly younger than Amory, had never had to catch up to anyone in size or energy or lungs. To Lucy, he seemed a giant. And his lungs were so famous that a Langdon neighbor had once offered him a quarter to yell as loud as he could. But when he was about to let out the yell, another neighbor had offered him fifty cents to keep still. Since he had collected from both, he had earned seventy-five cents just for keeping his mouth shut.

Amory was never as impressed by Ed as Lucy thought he should be. There was no feud between them, exactly, but Amory did keep reminding Ed about their difference in age, and Ed did keep reminding Amory about their difference in size. At best, it was an uneasy cousinship.

The talk turned finally from the cousins to the proposed circus and the battle between the Cave Men and the Stone Age Girls.

"Say," said Amory, changing the subject some, "if George and Ed and Len stay over until the sixth, they can be in the circus, too. Ed could give his Indian war whoop or his scream for help or both at once."

"It's much better if he sings." Mother saw a chance to avoid a little noise.

But Amory didn't hear her. He had finished his chocolate cake and was already going out through the shed, still planning. "And Len's nuts about chemistry, and I think he knows how to make stink bombs."

He was gone. Mother remained at the table to finish her cake, and Lucy sat quietly giving Topsy bits of cake under the big white tablecloth.

"Three more boys right now does seem a bit much, Harry," Mother said. "Effie and Charlie should get away now and then. And Gen shouldn't always have to be the big sister, but this may be more of a circus than I'd planned." She looked disturbed.

"A circus is a stroke of genius, Caroline," Father told her. "It keeps everybody out of mischief. And Amory and Ed are older now, so they shouldn't be so ambivalent."

"So what?" asked Lucy.

And then, of course, Father was off on his teaching. "That's another word for your vocabulary, Lucy. It means both liking and not liking someone. Don't you ever feel that way about anyone?"

"Yes, I do," Lucy said. "Now Gwen I like all the time, but with Gwin—sometimes I like her and sometimes I don't, especially when she tells what her father said about—" Lucy stopped just in time to avoid tattling on Mr. Owen.

*Three Cousins
for the Fourth of July*

As Father was leaving for the bank, he called, "Amory, Amory, Amory!" And when Amory stuck his head out of the cave, Father said, "Don't go off, will you? Stay put, for once. I want you to go down to the train to meet your cousins, and since it's Monday, the train will probably be late."

"Can I take them to see the blind pig?" Amory was talking as he ran toward the house. "Jerry and I can show them just how the raid went—I'll be the sheriff and Jerry can be Luke Morgan. And I'll yell, 'Open up, in the name of the Law!' "

"That Amory," Lucy said to herself, "he never heard the sheriff and I did, but it's already his raid." Then she thought a moment and decided he was welcome to it. She wanted nothing more to do with blind pigs or raids.

"You cannot go near the blind pig, Amory," Mother spoke in her once-and-for-all voice. "And come in and wash before you go to the depot, so you don't look like a pig yourself."

After Amory had disappeared underground again, Father came back into the kitchen and kissed Mother. "I know how things like that blind pig upset you, Caroline, but don't you worry about Amory growing up in Wales," he said. "Amory and his friends are so busy that they don't have time to hang around the wrong places. Why do you think I let them dig up the backyard for a hideout, right in sight of your back window?"

Then he kissed Mother again, and once more set off for the bank. So now Lucy knew that Mother also worried about Wales as a place for boys to grow up. Funny—until a few days ago, Lucy had only thought of Wales as her village, a dull place, perhaps, but never as a dangerous, wicked place.

Soon the girls and Edward were back, and they all set to work on the circus acts. Lucy wanted to add a hoop trick to Topsy's other stunts, but Topsy refused, time and again, to jump through the hoop unless it was resting on the floor. Lift it two inches, and Topsy either sat like a lump or she walked around the hoop to snatch the bit of food held as a reward on the other side.

So Lucy gave up and watched Guinnie and Edward practice their act. Mrs. Owen had sent over two huge white flour sacks. The children each stepped into one, and their sisters fastened them in so that only their heads stuck out. First they squatted down and then they slowly rose, and with Gwin's help they sang, *"I'm a little mushroom, growing in the rain."*

Gwen was covering two old straw hats with white paper for mushroom heads, but even so, Lucy had doubts about this act being exciting enough for a circus.

Gwen's act had not yet been decided, when suddenly she said, "Lucy, how about my doing the manual of arms? Right away, when Canada went to war, our teacher taught all our class the manual of arms."

Lucy hadn't the slightest idea what the manual of arms might be. Luckily, before she asked a stupid question, Gwin answered, "Wonderful, Gwen! You can borrow Amory's BB gun, and I'll bark out the orders, and before you begin, I'll sing 'The Maple Leaf Forever.' "

"I don't know about that," Lucy disagreed. "Seems to me when it's our barn and it's right here in North Dakota, we should sing 'The Star Spangled Banner.' "

"Oh, no," Gwin argued, "you're not at war!"

Before the argument was a full-scale battle, Gwen suggested a compromise. "Why not have us Canadians sing 'God Save the King' and you Americans sing 'My Country 'Tis of Thee,' all together. It's the same tune for both songs."

Everyone agreed, but Lucy made a mental note that since she couldn't sing any tune at all, she must tell the boys to bellow the American words at the tops of their lungs, or the King of England might win.

The train was so late that it was nearly time for the Owens to go home for supper when they heard the three long whistles at the crossing. Amory raced for the depot. Not long after that, back he came, carrying nothing, with Cousin Ed carrying a big suitcase, and Len lugging a huge cardboard box.

From the back gate, Ed saw Mother standing at the back door. "Hello, Aunt Caroline. Hello! Hello!" he shouted, each *Hello* louder than the one before.

Mother called to them, "Hello, Ed! Hello, Len!" But

in contrast to Ed, Mother sounded very faint. "Where's George? Didn't he come?" she asked.

By now the boys were at the house. There Len gently set down his big carton, as he said a polite, "Hello, Aunt Caroline."

"What do you know, Mother," Amory began, "George is downtown trying to sell *Saturday Evening Post* subscriptions, and he won a bike for what he sold in Langdon, and besides that, he's collecting junk, and he sells it for a lot of money because Europe needs scrap iron to fight the war and—"

The four Owens were staring at the two big brown-eyed Johnston cousins, so Ed interrupted Amory. "Where did you get all the pretty girls, Aunt Caroline, and an extra little boy, too?" It was like Ed to call the girls pretty, thought Lucy.

"The boy's name is Edward—just like yours, Ed," Lucy said, though as she said it, *Edward* and *Ed* seemed very different names. "And the girls are Gwendolyn, Gwinyth, and Guinevere Owen and they come from Canada." Lucy motioned toward each one as she spoke.

"Nice names—never heard of them before," Ed replied. "Oh, yes, I believe I did read about a queen named Guinevere, and didn't she come to a bad end, Aunt Caroline?" He grinned at Mother. This grin was what he and Amory had in common.

Mother now looked a second time at Len's box. "Something special in that box you're so careful about, Len? Bring it in, won't you?"

"You see, Aunt Caroline, because tomorrow's the Fourth of July," Len said, "Ed and I brought our carbide cannons. And when we got them all packed, we couldn't remember whether there's water in the little tank or not, and of course if the water mixes with the carbide—so maybe—" That was so long a speech for Len that he stopped there.

"You brought your carbide cannons?" Mother's voice showed her opinion of carbide cannons, the most powerful noisemakers ever invented for boys. Even Father considered them slightly dangerous and refused to buy one for Amory.

"Yup, and we brought plenty of carbide too!" shouted Ed. "And George sold his, so there's only two, and we won't shoot them until tomorrow morning." Then he misunderstood the look on Mother's face. "But we'll share them, Aunt Caroline. Honest we will. Amory can have just as many turns as we do."

The Owens now left for their supper, and Father and George came along the walk. "Well, well, well! You finally got here," boomed Father.

He started to carry Len's box into the house, but Mother blocked the doorway. "No, no, Harry! Leave that box out in the middle of the backyard. It's got two carbide cannons in it, and the boys can't remember whether or not they're ready to fire."

"Oh, cannons," said Father, sounding less startled than Mother but not very happy. "Boys, did your folks know you brought them with you?"

"We didn't lie, Uncle Harry," explained Len. "We just sort of didn't say anything."

"Anyway, we'd shot off all our firecrackers last week," Ed went on, "and we had to bring something for our share of the celebration, didn't we?"

So the box was left in the backyard during supper, and Lucy carefully kept Topsy in the house. Later Father suggested the box be shut in the stone house for the night. Amory made a great point of how ammunition was once stored in the most valuable marble building in Athens and "blew it up—all to smithereens!" He said it, of course, to make Lucy uneasy about her clubhouse, and Lucy knew it.

In the evening, after Ed and Len had inspected the cave with Amory, and the three of them were putting up the small white canvas tent to sleep in, Father and George sat on the front porch, talking. "How's business, George?" was Father's opening question. And he wasn't teasing. He was serious. It rang in Lucy's ears. "How's business, George?" It was unforgettable.

Early, early in the morning, just as dawn was beginning, Lucy was wakened by a series of shattering explosions. Not even a giant drum of gasoline, like the one that exploded last winter in the hardware store fire, could make such a deafening noise.

Then she remembered the Fourth of July and the carbide cannons—and she also remembered her stone house. She jumped from her bed to run downstairs. Mother was standing at the kitchen window, with her hair in a long heavy braid down her back and her kimono over her long nightgown. All Mother said to Lucy was, "The birthday of our country seems to have begun."

Near the stone house were Father and the four boys, but in a few minutes they were not alone. Through the gates and over the fence behind the barn came most of the boys in town and some of their fathers, too. They were not alarmed as Lucy had been, but the cannon shots so outdid any firecrackers that they were attracted, as Mother said later, "like flies to flypaper."

As the day went on, the cannon resounded, the big firecrackers banged, and the small red crackers popped one at a time for Edward and the girls and in whole bundles for Amory and the cousins. Only Father's specialty fireworks were left for evening.

Both Mother and a shuddering Topsy spent the day in the kitchen, Topsy behind the stove and Mother at the stove. The only time that Mother did go outdoors was to supervise the freezing of the ice cream. Father had to leave the firecrackers and dig deep into the damp icehouse sawdust for a dishpan of ice. This Rush Lake ice could never be put in a drink, of course, but the heavy blocks were cut and sledded into town every winter for the ice chest in the shed and for the ice-cream freezer.

The Fourth of July ice cream was always strawberry. Once Mother had poured the thick creamy mixture into the metal container and tightly fitted the dasher and the top, Father packed the wooden bucket around it with ice and rock salt. The rest was the children's work.

"Ladies first," Amory said. "Lucy, you turn it until you're tired. We boys will go to Jerry's for a while."

"No, siree!" Lucy refused. "A lady doesn't do all the work, unless you want me to get the lickings on all four of the dasher blades."

"What a piggish sister!" And Amory stuck out his tongue at her. But he stayed near the freezer and later took his turn cranking. Mother was called out three times to check it before she pronounced it done. Then she slowly pulled out the dasher, caked with pink ice cream and bits of red strawberries.

Lucy got first lick on one of the wooden blades, but as she pushed her tongue along it, some cream from the other blades drizzled down her best middy. And while she gazed sadly at the strawberry goo trickling down her front, she tipped the rest of the blades so they began to drip on her shoes.

"Luuuuuucy! You're wasting ours! Hand it over!" and Amory wrenched it away from her. Then Ed grabbed it from Amory. By the time they had struggled over their shares, most of the shares had dripped to the ground, by way of the boys' best shirts. And Len had not had any, not even a taste.

"Len, you go in and bring out a dish and a spoon," said Mother. "Let's have one person without strawberry flavored clothes."

But later, the two bigger boys raided Len's dish, and his whole helping slid down his shirtfront, leaving a wide trail of sticky pink.

Since it wasn't dark until late, Lucy was already very tired when she and the Owens lit their sparklers. Len managed the twirling phosphorus snakes, and the older boys sent up the Roman candles and zooming rockets in great sprays and showers across the wide black prairie sky.

But Lucy was waiting for the sailing of the three huge balloons of colored tissue paper. They were like enormous upside-down pears and as tall as Lucy herself. Underneath each one was a small cube of compressed hay. When Father decided the wind had died and the air was still, he shook open the first balloon and held it off the ground.

The cube was lighted and the heated air lifted the paper balloon, slowly at first and then faster and faster, higher and higher, until it was only a far-off spot of color. And finally it was gone, out of sight and far away.

Father bought only three of them each year, but Mother thought that three was three too many. While Lucy was gazing at the first beautiful lighted globe, slowly drifting away, Mother fussed about it as she did every Fourth of July.

"I don't think they're safe, Harry," Mother fretted. "Next year you simply must not order a single one."

"But they're really something for the children to remember always," Father answered. And Lucy knew
there would be balloons again next Fourth of July.

For Lucy, the Fourth meant these magical glowing
balloons, unlike anything else all the rest of the year.
Rising from the flat dusty field, they soared into the
night sky and floated to some distant spot, beyond the
Edge of Nowhere which Wales always seemed to be,
to a Somewhere she'd never seen.

Costumes and Quarrels

"Lucy, do an errand for me," Mother called from the foot of the stairs at eight o'clock the morning after the Fourth. "It's a truly beautiful day, dear, so get up soon." And Mother closed the stairway door before Lucy had time to ask, "Why can't Amory do the errand?"

Once downstairs, Lucy saw why the errand was hers. George was finishing his breakfast with Father, but the other three boys were still out in the tent, probably sound asleep.

"Please take this extra pan of hot cinnamon rolls over to the Dickermans," Mother said. "And if Hilda comes to the door and she has a few minutes, why not stay and talk a little with her? That is, if she wants to, poor little girl."

As Lucy carried the plate of rolls around the block,

she remembered it was barely a week since she'd carried another plate of food to hand to Hilda. And her own life had gone on, with the Owens, the new clubhouse, the cousins, the Fourth of July, and the circus plans. But Hilda's days—what must her life have been like?

At the Dickermans' back door, Lucy noticed that the messy backyard was entirely cleaned up. Not a single tin can, bottle or piece of rusty machinery remained. Mother thought everyone had only talked, but someone had worked.

Almost as soon as Lucy knocked, Hilda was at the door. She looked exactly as she had before. Somehow Lucy had expected her to change.

"Oh, sticky buns! I love them!" Hilda said softly. Of course, a girl could still like sticky buns after her baby brother died, yet it did surprise Lucy.

"Pa and the twins are over at Kinsers', and Ma's still asleep," Hilda continued in her whisper. "Want to see the new baby?"

"I'd love to," answered Lucy. And she did want to see him, very much. Ever since she'd heard he was a seven-month baby, she'd puzzled about his looks.

"We mustn't wake Ma," Hilda warned as she tip-toed into the kitchen ahead of Lucy. There, on two straight chairs, placed front to front, was a small card-board carton not much larger than a big shoe box. Peering over the side, Lucy saw that it was lined with cotton, just as Mother had said. And under a fuzzy blue blanket was the new baby, though all Lucy could see was the tiny head with no hair, the eyes squeezed shut, no eyebrows or eyelashes, a flat little nose, and a mouth that seemed too small to open.

"Mrs. Sanderson is coming today to give him his first real bath," whispered Hilda.

"You mean he hasn't had a bath yet?" queried Lucy in a shocked tone.

"No, he's special," answered Hilda. "But he's nice, isn't he?" And Hilda looked at him so lovingly that Lucy tried to admire him. Now and then she had gone with Mother to see new babies, but this one with his homely squeezed-up face was almost too new.

"Yes, he's very nice," agreed Lucy. "My mother says he'll always be special to her, too, because she didn't think he'd live."

"I know," said Hilda. "I know. Your ma was awful good that day—"

To keep Hilda from going back to that day, Lucy broke in. "Has he got a name yet, Hilda?"

"Yah. Ma's set on calling him Charlie, cause it sounds so much like Karlie."

"But I think my father told me that Karl and Charles are the same name," Lucy said. "Karl is Charles in German, isn't it?"

"How could they be the same? They aren't spelled the same," Hilda insisted in her whisper. "And besides, your pa isn't a German so how could he know about German names?"

"He used to be a college prof—" Lucy stopped, remembering Mother had told her that farmers might not do business with a professor. "Well, it's true," Lucy said. "Those names are spelled different, but they do sound alike, don't they? Baby Charlie—I like that name."

Having satisfied Hilda about the name, Lucy tiptoed back to the door, where she invited Hilda to the circus. "Do you think you and Rudolph and Adolph could come over to our barn tomorrow afternoon to a circus we're putting on? It's not much of a circus, really," Lucy explained. "Amory's going to do some magic, and my dog Topsy can do tricks, and my Johnston cousins from Langdon are going to do something special, and—"

"I'd like to come. I really would, and I'll bring the twins." Hilda was excited for a moment. Then she turned housekeeper and slipped the warm rolls off the Johnstons' plate and onto one of their own. Handing the plate back to Lucy, Hilda said, "Take yours back, will you? At our house everything gets busted."

Perhaps because she now felt better about the Dickermans, Lucy noticed on the way home that Mother was right about the weather. "It's a truly beautiful day." Lucy repeated Mother's words. The sky was full of puffy white clouds, the pink clover in the ditch was in bloom, and the air tasted good, right down into your lungs. Sometimes Wales seemed so perfect that she didn't care whether those city cousins laughed at it or not.

By now the boys had piled into the dining room to eat their way through big dishes of oatmeal, plates of pancakes and syrup, and cup after cup of cocoa. While the boys ate, Lucy asked about the circus she had missed.

"I didn't see it, and George didn't either," said Ed. "Len went twice, didn't you, Len?"

"Yup," said Len, who never wore out his vocabulary with overuse.

"Ed, how could you stay home with a circus in town?" asked Lucy.

"Oh, we were both there, but we didn't exactly see it," said Ed, laughing. "George had a job watering the animals. And a regular barker had a sore throat, so I hired out to yell in front of a sideshow. Want to hear how I sounded?" And before Mother could stop him, Ed bellowed, "Step right up, folks! Come see the world's fattest woman and the Siamese twins and the living skeleton and the—"

Mother hurried in with fresh pancakes. "Here, Ed," she interrupted. "Try these—just off the griddle." And Ed, with an appetite like Amory's, stopped barking to pour on syrup and stow away more pancakes.

"Was she really the world's fattest woman and were the Siamese twins really joined?" Lucy questioned all such impossible things, but at the same time she hoped they were true.

"Bet they were all fakes," said Amory.

Three pancakes later, Ed explained. "The fat woman was awful fat, but she might have had some kind of pink pillows on her, too. And I couldn't be sure, but it looked to me as though the Siamese twins only wore one dress with four sleeves and two holes for their heads. But I never could figure out that skeleton man. Boy, was he thin! He was a real skeleton!"

Len, who had been eating as steadily as Amory and Ed, said, "Something wrong with his chemistry."

Lucy started to say, "He had chemistry?" Then she knew the boys would laugh at her. But she had always thought of people and chemistry as two different things.

Chemistry brought her back to the circus plans. "Did Amory tell you we're putting on a circus tomorrow in the barn?" Lucy asked. "Won't you both be in it—please?"

Len nodded and continued to consume pancakes. Ed, who saw the circus was important to her, winked and said, "Sure. Want me for a barker?" And once more he began to bellow, "Step up, folks! Come see Little Lucy, the littlest red-haired girl in the state!" Topsy came in just then, so Ed yelled even louder, "And here's her ferocious wild dog with fangs two inches long!" The noise was enough to make Lucy cover her ears.

Soon Amory began the day's trapping plans. "Stan

and Jerry will be here any minute. The farmers are going crazy with the gophers eating all their grain this year, and I've got traps for everybody to have one. And should I take my BB gun?"

"NO GUNS!" Mother spoke from the kitchen in a voice that nearly equaled Ed's. "That BB gun stays right here in the kitchen."

"And anyway, Gwen needs it to practice her manual of arms," Lucy added.

"A girl doing the manual of arms?" asked Mother. "Honestly, I can never be sure what the Owens will come up with next."

Fearing Mother might mention Gwin's hula, Lucy quickly changed the subject. "Gwin's going to sing. Won't you sing something, too, Ed?" Lucy begged. Ed wasn't all bellow. He had a wonderful voice and loved music.

"Sure, I'll sing," Ed agreed. "And what'll Len do?"

"We thought Len might do a chemistry trick," Lucy said.

"I'll do one," Len answered.

"Please, before you go off for all day, tell me what you need for costumes. Jerry and Stan said they don't need any. Do any of you?" Lucy asked.

"Nope," said Len, with his mouth full of cinnamon roll.

"I sure do," Amory said. "A magician can't wear ordinary clothes. I've got to have a long coat. Hey, Mother," he called to the kitchen, "how about that old black suit in the upstairs closet?"

"Why, Amory, that's the suit your father wore when we were married." Mother sounded shocked.

Amory always had an answer. "Well, he's not planning to get married again, is he? And when you shook it out last spring, you said it had a moth hole, so even if he does get married again, I think—"

"Oh, you might as well wear it, Amory." Mother gave in. "Run upstairs and bring it down."

"But, Aunt Caroline, if I'm going to sing, I need that black coat worse than Amory does," Ed objected. And before you could blink your eye, Ed was pounding up the stairs after Amory. In two seconds there were roars and bangs and thumps in the bedroom overhead, and then a rush pell-mell down the stairs, ending with a crash as the two boys fell the last few steps, cushioned only by Father's suit.

By now Ed and Amory were rolling in such a tangle of legs and arms and black broadcloth sleeves and coat-tails that Mother didn't even try to separate them.

Instead she raised her voice to its highest pitch. "Boys!" she screeched. "Let go of that coat!" And when they continued to grapple in coattails and coat sleeves, Mother yanked the first sleeve she could reach, and Lucy gripped the other one. Both of them jerked at the same moment. There was a loud sound of ripping, and Mother and Lucy each held a sleeve, while Amory and Ed still fought in the remains of the coat.

"Stop it!" Mother screamed one last time.

And everything stopped—the yelling stopped, the hitting stopped, and the wrestling stopped.

"Now get up off that floor, both of you," Mother commanded. "I'll stitch the sleeves back in this coat and tomorrow you boys will take turns wearing it. Get your traps and your paper bags of sandwiches, and off—you—go!"

"Okay," said Amory meekly, as they all hurried toward the front door. "Okay, but it sure is a shame Lucy tore that good coat." He didn't wait to hear Lucy howl at him. In five seconds, he and the cousins had joined Jerry and Stan, and the five boys set off across the ploughed field as fast as they could run.

When Lucy began to sputter, Mother said, "You go right out to your clubhouse and work on your circus. Don't bother to help me this morning. All I want is a little quiet, please." And Mother looked so cross that Lucy ran out the back door as fast as the boys had run out the front one.

The rest of the morning the girls worked on costumes. Gwen sewed old brass buttons on a jacket for her uniform, and Gwin sewed an American flag and a Canadian flag on a white sheet. This was to hang behind the "My Country 'Tis of Thee" "God Save the King" act.

Since no one was sure what a dog trainer should wear, Lucy repaired Topsy's outfit for tricks, sewing fresh pink ribbons on her doll bonnet and a few inches of white lace around the pale blue silk cape. Topsy seemed to like the bonnet, but she did not like the cape. Yet Lucy felt that, especially for a circus, the cape made all the difference between an ordinary dog walking a few steps on her hind legs and Topsy waltzing five or six steps in a circle.

Soon Edward and Guinnie began to quarrel over their costumes. How could any child quarrel over flour sacks? Lucy couldn't believe her ears.

"Guinnie's sack is better than mine. Mine's got a hole in it," whimpered Edward, as he began to stamp inside his sack. And he jumped and tugged and tugged and jumped until there was another sound of ripping. Then Lucy lost her temper.

"Edward Albert Christian Owen, you stop that! You're behaving like a brat!" Lucy screeched as loud as Mother had. And Edward, surprised at anyone's screeching at him, stopped his stamping and began to weep. His crying sounded heartbroken and abused, as though Lucy had hit him.

His three sisters knelt down beside him, wiped his tears, and comforted him. "You can have my sack, poor boy," offered Guinnie.

"There, there, Edward, don't you cry." And Gwen patted him and eased him out of his sack.

"We won't let Lucy hurt our little Edward," Gwin said, as though Lucy were a big bully.

By that time Lucy had begun to feel apologetic, even guilty. But before she could say a word, Edward, out of his flour sack, came at her, butting his head in her stomach and kicking her in the shins.

"Ouch!" Lucy yelped. "Quit that! You're hurting me!" And though Gwen and Gwin pulled him away, Lucy could see that they thought their angelic Edward was not to blame.

At that moment, Mother's call to come set the table probably saved the circus. Edward set off for home, dragging Guinnie's sack in the dust. But as he left, he picked up a stone and heaved it toward the girls' clubhouse.

Edward was always so far from hitting anything he aimed at that the girls thought him very funny. "That's our squire," hooted Gwen. "He leaves no stone unturned, does he?" And again they were a club, all laughing together.

But Lucy's shins were still tingling as she went in to help Mother. And she wondered when Edward would be big enough for her to kick in return.

George was the only cousin at dinner, and he seemed interested when Father asked, "How's the biggest circus —well, not in the world, but in Wales?"

"A circus!" said George. "Want me to draw up some advertising signs so you'll have a big crowd? I'll bet I could make people come from all over."

"I'll bet you could, George—droves of them," said Mother, laughing. "But this is a very small circus and not a very big barn. So I'm doing the advertising, just phoning the mothers who might want to bring their children."

"If you don't advertise, Lucy, you won't make much, will you?" George commented. "How much are you charging?"

"We haven't decided," said Lucy. "Maybe you could help us, George. You're so good at business."

"I know what you could do," he answered. "Cash, even pennies, might be hard for some kids to scrape up. Why not have everybody bring a piece of junk for admission?"

"Good idea," Father agreed. "Every backyard in this village needs junk cleared out. The only thing is," Father paused, "I don't want all the junk in Wales dumped in my backyard. You promise to get it out of here before too long?"

"Don't you worry, Uncle Harry. Junk is money now," George said. "Maybe my folks would even take a little of it home in their auto when they come tomorrow night to get us."

"Load your folks' new auto with junk? Are you out of your mind?" George saw Father's point.

By late afternoon, all the boys were back from their hunt. After eating a whole jar full of Mother's brown-sugar cookies, they began to rehearse. Ed practiced singing "On the Road to Mandalay," and he also listened over and over again to the record of a long poem called "Boots." It was about a soldier who went mad because all he saw in front of him were boots, marching up and down.

Mother wanted Ed to stick to singing, but she finally agreed to his reciting two stanzas of "Boots" if he wasn't too loud.

Len didn't have his chemistry set with him, but he promised he'd find some chemistry somewhere for his trick. Then Amory tried on the long black coat, with the two sleeves sewn back in. And though the back tails dragged on the floor and the sleeves had to be turned up three times, Amory pronounced it perfect for hiding magic equipment.

Jerry and Stan said they were keeping their acrobatics a surprise. As it turned out, their acrobatics weren't the only circus surprise.

The Circus
in the Barn

By afternoon of the next day, one end of the barn was swept, boxes for the children and chairs for the women were set in rows, and at a table outside the barn door, Amory and George stood ready to collect the junk admission.

"If you like, I'll appraise the stuff," George said to Amory.

"How much a pound will you pay?" Amory asked.

"Well, it's really for a war effort, so maybe it could be a donation? I could manage it for you," George said.

"The USA isn't at war, so no donations." Amory was quick to refuse.

Then George promised. "I'll figure the best price I can, and your two clubs can have the profits."

Soon the mothers began to appear. Mrs. Fischer brought Robbie, who carried a big rusty skillet for his admission. Mrs. Bortz came with two small grandsons, dragging a heavy iron pump between them. Mrs. Bortz grinned at Lucy. "You see—more boys. Always I get more boys!"

Sarah Lowenstein brought her little brother Davy, as spoiled a boy as Edward. Sarah handed over an old ax-head, explaining the men had used it when their store burned. "Now Mama hates to see it around."

Mrs. Flint led in Morrie and Dorrie, bringing two flatirons wrapped in tissue paper so no one would get dirty. Mrs. Flint put each child on a chair and then sat on a chair herself. Lucy looked at Mother, and Mother looked at Lucy, as though she meant, "It's your circus, Lucy. You're in charge."

So Lucy went over to Mrs. Flint and said rather timidly, "I'm sorry, Mrs. Flint, but the children have to sit on boxes. The chairs are just for mothers."

"Well, if you've got very clean boxes," Mrs. Flint replied, "I can put down a handkerchief on the box Dorrie sits on." So the two young Flints were "boxed" like all the rest of the children, only not quite like all the rest.

Mrs. Schnitzler had been invited, and Mother had the boys lift out an especially wide mahogany chair for her. But Mrs. Schnitzler confused the chair with the box next to it, sat on the apple crate, and the splintering sound was horrendous. Mother gasped, and then saw it wasn't the chair, only the crate. Everyone probably thought Mother's gasp was sympathy for Mrs. Schnitzler, but Lucy suspected it was really Mother's alarm for her favorite chair.

Hilda and Mrs. Sanderson brought Rudolph and

Adolph. In brand-new blue shirts and overalls, both boys were shining clean, from their bare feet up to their tow hair. "Stan brought my admission this morning—that bundle of leftover metal roofing," Mrs. Sanderson reminded Amory, "and now I can't stay more than to look in and say hello to everybody. The new baby might need me."

The Dickermans offered a very long wire for their junk. At first George said he couldn't appraise one wire very highly, especially for three children. "Wire's okay, for them, they've just moved here," Lucy said quickly.

Then Lucy led the three of them to front-row boxes, because it was their first Wales event. The four Scheler boys, like four steps in size, each brought a heavy stove lid, really good junk, not even rusty. George appraised the four lids the highest of all.

Three young Kinsers came with their mother. Their junk was all different metals—a battered copper pan, a wagon wheel rim, and the brass ring from a carriage lamp. Lucy saw to it that Mrs. Kinser had a very big chair near the door, since Mother had said that morning, "Mrs. Kinser may not be able to come. She's expecting any minute, but I told her to come anyway."

Mrs. Owen slipped in at the side door, in her quiet, gentle way. She had been soothing Edward about his flour sack and carefully brushing his hair, though it couldn't possibly matter under his mushroom hat.

Because their flour sacks were hot and tight, Guinnie and Edward began the circus. Gwen and Gwin half lifted, half shoved them out to the cleared space in front. Then while Gwin sang with them, they first squatted down and then gradually grew to full height, endlessly singing, "*I'm a little mushroom, growing in the rain.*" Everyone applauded, though it was obvious that the two older Scheler boys thought it wasn't worth a stove lid.

After the girls had untied the sacks and emptied the children out of them, Ed came on stage in the long black coat to sing *"On the road to Mandalay, where the flying fishes play."* Everyone clapped so hard for this solo that Ed bowed and kept on bowing, which made people feel they must keep on clapping.

This went on as long as Amory could stand it. Then he called out impatiently, "Hey, Ed, quit the bowing and get into the boots!" So Ed reached into a front-row box and dragged out Father's black rubber hip boots. This was a surprise costume.

Quickly Ed pulled them on, stood up, and began pounding to and fro across the floor, reciting, "Boots, marching up and down again, boots," each word louder than the last. After the first stanza, he was into the mood of the mad poem, but he couldn't remember any more words. So he thumped and banged harder and harder as he marched, and he yelled louder and louder. "Boots! BOOTS! BOOOOTS!" He was like a needle stuck in a record.

"Boots! BOOTS! BOOOOTS!" he thundered out. The mothers began to look jittery, the smaller children were terrified, and the old barn floor began to shake. But Ed pounded on. "Boots!" He began all over again. "BOOTS!"

Only Amory could turn Ed off. "Ed!" Amory screamed above the "Boots!" "Ed, you're hogging the black coat! It's my turn to wear it!" Amory bellowed. The spell of the mad soldier was broken, and Ed laughed as hard as anyone.

After all those "Boots!" a waltzing dog seemed very tame, but Topsy looked so fetching in her lace-edged cape and her bonnet tied under her chin that people appreciated her as much as Lucy thought they should.

Topsy still refused to jump through the hoop, so Lucy excused her. Then with Topsy on one knee and the upright hoop on the other, Lucy sat down to enjoy the rest of the circus.

Gwin now sang her solo. "It's a war song that the British soldiers sing at the Front," Gwin announced. "And the name of it is 'It's a Long Way to Tipperary.'" And Gwin began to sing. Gwin was always like a different person when she sang in her high sweet voice. Lucy could understand why Mother often said, "Gwin sings like an angel," though both Mother and Lucy knew that Gwin was no angel.

In the applause afterward, Lucy looked around and saw that even Mrs. Bortz, with her enemy German soldier nephews, was clapping loudly for Gwin's "Tipperary."

Amory had barely come to the stage in Father's long black coat when the circus was interrupted by a screech. Mrs. Scheler, in her Mother-Hubbard kitchen dress and huge calico apron, stood at the barn door.

"Who stole my stove lids? Where's my kids? Who done that trick on me?" she bawled. "I go to start my range for supper, and there ain't a stove lid on it, and Joe says the kids took all four. I'll have all of youse arrested for stealing."

She might have gone on and on, but by that time she had noticed mothers there as well as children, and she quieted down a bit. "Anyway, I got to have them lids, and my kids got to carry them home. And they stay home, too!" And she disappeared from the doorway.

Lucy looked out and saw her grab her stove lids and thrust one at each of her four boys. "You kids—hit for home—now git!" were the last words they heard from her. So part of the audience was gone, and so was part of the pile of scrap metal.

Amory shook his head, and he started his act. "Ladies and gents, you see I've nothing in my hands and nothing up my sleeves," and he turned his hands to and fro and shook Father's coat sleeves. "Now I'll make a magic pass over this one red ball," he continued, "and now watch very carefully—I shall produce two more balls for you, one blue and one yellow."

Sure enough, the blue one appeared right after the magic gesture, but there was trouble with the yellow one. Amory jiggled and juggled and squirmed inside the coat, and he finally said, "Well, I'll try again, slow day for magic."

So he started all over again. This time he shook himself and the coat so violently that a yellow ball dropped out from under his arm and bounced away into the audience. By that time he could only laugh and blame Mother. "I've lost this trick. My Mother needs to mend my father's coat with a little magic." And he grinned at Mother. Then he said, "I'll skip the rabbit trick. But you wait until next year's circus. Rabbits multiply, you know, so by next summer there might be oodles of rabbits."

Stan and Jerry came out for their acrobatics. Jerry first turned three cartwheels in a row. Next he flipped over and stood on his head until he turned not only red but an alarming purple. Everyone clapped loudly, the children in admiration and the mothers hoping he'd soon stand up and change to a normal color.

Once Jerry was back on his feet, Stan brought in a small stool. Standing against the wall, with the stool beside him, Stan helped Jerry climb up until he had a foot on each of Stan's broad shoulders. And there Jerry stood, not holding on to anything. Everyone *Oh*ed and *Ah*ed at this, though as Amory said later, it wasn't exactly earthshaking.

This was when the circus should have ended, for the rest was a total disaster. It began with Topsy. Kinsers' cat had been prowling for mice in the old cowshed attached to the barn, and she now came ambling across the stage floor. One sniff of cat, and Topsy jumped high in the air, gave a tremendous leap through the hoop that Lucy was still holding, and then with bonnet strings and blue silk cape flying out behind her, Topsy was gone.

Before Lucy could rush off to catch her, the Canadian and American flags were brought in and everyone had to stand up at attention, while Gwin led them in "My Country 'Tis of Thee," or rather, the boys shouted "My Country 'Tis of Thee," and the Owens sang "God Save the King."

While this was going on, Gwen stood at attention, and in her brass-buttoned jacket she did look very military. Then she followed Gwin's sharp commands, lowering, shouldering, pointing Amory's BB gun. Of course, Mother had checked to be sure there wasn't a BB within a mile of it. But as Gwin barked the order, "Ready, aim, FIRE!" and Gwen fired, the most awful thundering shot went off.

The Flints screamed—all three of them. Davy Lowenstein jumped on Sarah's lap and hid his face. And Mother looked as though she'd been shot in the stomach. Even Amory seemed dazed, until he looked around and saw that Ed was missing.

"The carbide cannon!" yelled Amory. And Ed came through the side door, bowing and smiling as though he expected applause. Instead every single mother scolded him, the girls booed, and Edward even tried a rude noise. Ed had spoiled a very impressive act, Lucy thought.

Len's was the last act on the circus program. He came forward and announced, "In my hand I hold some chemistry. I throw it on the floor, and this is what you get."

And what did they get? A stink bomb! The stink rose and spread out the barn door, and so did the audience. Len slipped out the side door and escaped before anyone else.

Gradually people said thank-you and went off toward their homes. All that was left of the circus was a heap of scrap. "It's worth about fifty cents," said George. "If you divide that among the two clubs and Len and Ed— let me see," and he did the arithmetic in his head. "That'll be five cents each. Aunt Caroline, maybe you'd like to advance the cash to them, and then when I've sold the junk, I'll reimburse you."

"Reimburse," Lucy repeated to herself, thinking George must have been born with those money words in his head.

Mother found eight nickels in her handbag, enough for everyone except Lucy and Amory. "You two wait until your father comes home," Mother said. "He'll be glad to pay you, now that you've stopped fighting and have a truce."

"Truce? My eye!" exclaimed Amory. "That was just a circus truce."

"Oh, Amory," Mother said dolefully, but she said no more. She probably hadn't expected peace for very long anyway.

Late that evening Uncle Charlie and Aunt Effie drove up to the house in their seven-passenger Hudson. Uncle

Charlie was heavier than Father and had an even temper, totally different from Father's quick one. But he had the same loud voice. Aunt Effie was more beautiful than Mother, with big brown eyes, a head of short golden curls, and the energy of three ordinary women.

They didn't stay long, only long enough to ask whether the boys had behaved themselves. Mother insisted they had been no trouble at all. "We've had the Fourth and a trapping expedition and a circus in the barn, and they've been invaluable in everything," she said.

"Couldn't have got along without them," Father added.

Aunt Effie said, "Well then, get along into the auto, boys."

And Uncle Charlie, who mostly echoed Aunt Effie, said, "Yes, boys, get along into the auto. We've twenty miles to go."

Once in the Hudson, Aunt Effie leaned out and said, "Thank you, Caroline. I knew they wouldn't get into any mischief here with you and Harry."

And Uncle Charlie echoed, "And I knew if they did get into mischief, you'd know what to do." And off they drove to Langdon.

Mother and Father sat down on the porch swing, and as they slowly moved to and fro, Mother said, "Know what to do—indeed. What do you do with carbide cannons and stink bombs?" Then she laughed softly and said to Father, "But I wouldn't have it any other way. Some things Amory and Lucy may not have, but they're rich in cousins."

The Escaped Prisoner

S ummer's nearly over," Father said, as he sat down to Saturday dinner. It was a quiet noon, since Amory had gone with Stan to spend the night at the Schneiders' farm, where Stan's father was working.

"Nearly over? What do you mean?" asked Mother. "Why, we just had the Fourth of July."

"Yes, but the transients are already beginning to come," Father explained. "There's a small camp of them down by the tracks. I hear there was a knife fight there last night."

"Goodness! That's all Wales needs," Mother said unhappily.

"Well, since there's no work in the fields yet, sooner or later they'll be coming to the back door for handouts," Father went on. "That's okay, but have the hoe handy by the back door and see that they work before you feed them."

Lucy never talked about it, but she was always a little afraid at this time of year. Often these wandering men left the railroad tracks that they followed from town to town and came along the road past the Johnstons' house. Not only were they strangers, but they looked strange. The old men walked doggedly by, often with sacks slung over their backs. The younger men often walked in pairs, but all, of course, wore dusty old clothes and looked very different from the village men or the farmers.

"This makes me wonder," Mother said thoughtfully. "Lucy was going with me to the Ladies Aid out at Cochrans', but Gwinyth and Guinevere both have sore throats so Gwendolyn's staying home with them and Lucy wants to stay home alone."

"If it's the transients you're worrying about, Caroline, she'll be all right here," Father replied. "I doubt if Lucy will get into a knife fight." Father chuckled. "Anyway, that fierce police dog, Miss Topsy, will protect her."

Topsy, at the mention of her name, came out from under the table and began pawing Lucy's lap for a bite of biscuit. "Here's one nonworker that never has to try hard for a handout," said Father, as he gave Topsy a morsel of cheese.

At two o'clock, when the Quimbys came with Mrs. Owen and Edward, Mother again asked Lucy, "Don't you want to come? There's room for you."

But as Lucy thought of an afternoon at the Ladies Aid, passing plates and watching over Edward and seeing all the best cakes disappear, while she and the smaller children got the soggiest salmon sandwiches and the leftover slushy jello, she chose an afternoon with

Topsy—transients or no.

"Well, it's nicer for your father if you stay," Mother said. "I can't get home until after supper. You get the Saturday beans and brown bread out of the oven and on the table for him, and don't forget the fresh rhubarb pie." Mother gave her a kiss and went out to the waiting auto.

For a long time Lucy sat in her clubhouse, rocking and reading the July *Saint Nicholas* from cover to cover. By four o'clock she thought of going indoors for a cookie. But as she raised her eyes from the page, all thoughts of a cookie vanished.

At the open door of the clubhouse stood a transient. She first saw his dusty shoes, scuffed old farm shoes. Then she quickly looked up to the man's face. He was young and he didn't look like a tramp, but his jacket and overalls were dirty and very wrinkled.

"Hello," Lucy said. Topsy got up and barked "*Worf!*" in her sharp voice, at the same time wagging her short tail. "Can't be too bad a man," Lucy said to herself, "if Topsy wags her tail." Then she remembered Topsy wasn't old enough to have lived through a transient season, so she might not be a reliable guide.

"Hello," the young man answered Lucy. "Your pa's not home, is he?" And he asked it as though he hoped Father was not at home. It was not a reassuring question.

So Lucy protected herself with a mild fib. "I expect him home with Mother very soon," she lied. "If you want to see him, he's down at the bank."

"So your ma's not home either?" the man went on.

And of course, Lucy had already let on that Mother wasn't home. So she didn't even answer, just rocked, with Topsy close by.

"If you're home alone, could you get me something

to eat?" he asked next. "And I'd sure like a drink of cold well water. Got a cup I could use?"

Since he was staring into the stone house, he naturally saw the orange-and-white cups of Mother's old tea set on the clubhouse shelf. So Lucy picked up a cup and handed it to him. Then she led the way to the pump. Surely there was nothing wrong with giving a man a free drink of water.

He pumped while she held the cup, and he drank and drank.

"Sure was thirsty," he remarked when he finally handed the cup back to her. "And I'm gol-darn hungry too. Not a bite to eat since yesterday. Your folks wouldn't mind if you gave me something to eat, do you think?" and he smiled at her. Really, he had a very nice smile, Lucy had to admit.

But the Johnston rule was "No work, no eat." So Lucy moved toward the back shed door, where the hoe leaned. Picking it up to hand to him, she said, "I can't feed you until—here's our hoe."

He backed away. "Not going to take a hoe to me, are you?" he asked. "And if you won't feed me until your folks get home, I won't get fed at all. I've got to mosey along. I got to cross the border into Canada tonight."

"Oh, I wasn't going to take the hoe to you," Lucy said. "But it's my father's rule about handouts that men have to work in the garden first."

"Just this once, your father's wrong," the man insisted. "I know your father, and I knew this was his place when I came in the front gate."

"How could you know it's our place? You've never been in our yard before. And how do you know my father? And who are you, anyway?" Lucy spilled it all out at once, and piece by piece he answered it.

"I spotted your five big cottonwoods," he began, "and before, when I drove into town, somebody told me those trees belonged to your folks."

"You've been in Wales before?" Lucy asked.

"Yup, and I'll tell you some more, if you'll give me a plate of something to eat. Here I stand starving and you hang onto a hoe and ask me questions." He smiled at her again. "Not very nice of you!"

"Tell me your name, though," Lucy kept on. "It's not fair, when you know our name, to keep your own name a secret."

"Look, little girl, my name is a secret, but if I tell you who I am, will you help me and not tell your pa and your ma I've been here? And mostly would you please feed me?"

Lucy still clutched the hoe, but she leaned against the screen door, more or less at ease, as she said, "Tell me first who you are, and then I'll decide."

"You're a really tough character," the young man said, laughing. "All right—I'm Luke Morgan. And yesterday I escaped from the Langdon county jail."

"You're Luke Morgan!" Lucy exclaimed. "My folks felt awful about your being put in jail."

"Now I'm out. I think the sheriff wanted me to escape. Yesterday afternoon my cell door wasn't locked, and a back window was open too. So I just climbed out and hid behind a hedge until dark. Along about dusk a new guard came on, and lying there I could hear him talking to somebody about searching for me out at my uncle's."

Luke paused in his story and scowled. "But that's one place I'll never go to again—not on your life!"

"But what will you do?" Lucy asked. "Should I phone

my father to come help you?"

"No. Your father likes me and he might want to help, but he'd have to turn me in. He has to be very legal. All bankers have to be. You can see that, can't you?" Luke spoke seriously. "You'll only put me back in jail if you tell anyone. Now you know who I am, but this has to be between you and me."

"Where can you go? You can't hide on the prairie— nobody can. There's no place to get out of sight," Lucy said.

"You feed me something, and I'll get out of sight," Luke answered.

As Lucy put down the hoe and opened the screen door, Luke started to follow her. "Oh, you can't come in," she told him. "My folks wouldn't want that." She stood in the half-open door, thinking where he might go. "How about my bringing you some food in my clubhouse?"

"You mean that little stone outhouse?" and Luke pointed to it.

"It's not an outhouse. It's my clubhouse," Lucy corrected him.

"Okay, it's a clubhouse. But don't you go indoors and forget me. And don't you phone your pa, either," and Luke went toward the clubhouse while Lucy went to the kitchen.

She opened the warm oven and pulled out the pot of baked beans and heaped a plate with them. Then she opened the tin of brown bread and slipped the loaf out so she could cut off nearly half of it. She covered the beans and the bread and shoved them back in the oven. As she went past the icebox in the shed, she put a big chunk of butter on the plate also. Topsy, thinking this was an extra dinner, stayed very near her as Lucy

carried the food to the stone house.

Looking inside, she saw no sign of Luke. She started to call, "Luke!" Then she realized that a man in hiding doesn't want to be hailed, even if it's to be fed. So she simply stepped inside, and there was Luke standing stiff with his back against the wall beside the door, so that until you were inside, you didn't see him.

"Good girl," said Luke. "Ordinarily, I'm not partial to beans, but right now—and doesn't your family use forks, even for beans?"

Lucy laughed. "I'll get you a fork. Have you got a jackknife to spread your bread?"

"Jails don't let you have a knife," Luke said.

"I suppose not," Lucy answered. "I really don't know much about jails." And with Topsy at her heels, she ran to the kitchen for a table knife and fork and a bottle of catsup.

When she got back, Luke was rubbing the butter on the brown bread and stuffing his mouth with it. "Ummmmm," he said, "I think I was the hungriest man in the States. And catsup—good!" He talked as though he felt he should be polite to her. "You like to cook and keep house?"

"Well, I'm in no hurry to begin," Lucy answered. Then she asked in a worried way, "Can't you tell me what you'll do next?"

Luke stopped eating a moment. "Say, what's your name besides Johnston?"

"It's Lucy," she told him. "And once my father told me that Luke and Lucas are almost twin names to mine."

"Really? We don't look much alike though, do we?" Luke grinned. "And now what's for dessert? I'm still starved, but you can't eat more than a certain amount of beans."

"How about rhubarb pie? My mother makes awfully good rhubarb pie," Lucy bragged.

"Okay. And you got a piece of cheese to go with it?"

So once more Lucy ran to the kitchen with Topsy leading the way this time. Back at the clubhouse with half a pie, Lucy watched Luke down it faster than Amory could. And as she saw it disappear, Lucy wondered how she'd explain the loss of half a pie.

Meantime, Luke sat, his feet stretched nearly out the door. "Now I'm fed, I find I'm one tired man," he said, "and there's not room to stretch out here. Anyway —somebody might come here." While he was eating, he hadn't seemed like an escaped prisoner, but now he looked scared. "Lucy, how about my napping in your barn?"

"Oh, my father's even more strict about strangers in the barn," Lucy hastily said. "People light a match and go to sleep and the barn burns up, or they fall out of the loft and break their bones—or well, anyway my father locks it every night, because that's where he keeps our auto."

"That's enough reasons. Okay. I won't sleep in your barn. But I can't sleep in this little out—I mean little clubhouse. After it's real dark, I can walk around the town and head north. I'll be over the border before it's light, but now—where do I sleep?" Luke obviously expected her to solve his problem.

"I almost forgot. You're Canadian, aren't you? And if you cross the border, you're safe, aren't you?" Lucy kept forgetting it was sleep he wanted most.

"I'm so dog-tired after not sleeping those nights in jail and walking all last night that I've got to sleep before I set out on the last miles," Luke explained.

"In jails, don't they let you sleep?" Lucy was fascinated by these glimpses of jail life.

"You can sleep—if you can. But they hadn't cleared out the bedbugs from the last prisoner, so I sat up in a straight chair every night. Bedbugs aren't chair bugs, you know."

Lucy wanted to ask him more about jails, but he began to look very drowsy. "My brother Amory's cave is empty. He's away for overnight, and my folks don't go down into that," Lucy said.

"A cave in this yard? How come?" asked Luke.

"My father says boys get into less trouble if they have a hideout, and this town's quite rough."

"Yeah! You can't tell me anything about this dump of a town!" exclaimed Luke. "Look what happened to me!"

Though Lucy understood why Luke felt that way, she had to stand up for Wales when anyone called it a dump. "You see, Luke," she began, "I was born here so it's my hometown."

"I know how you feel. Now I come from Pilot Mound in Manitoba, and lots of people might think that was a dump. But I'll be so glad to see it that I'll—" then Luke interrupted himself. "And where do I sleep in your beautiful little country village?"

Lucy laughed. "You joke just the way my father does. I wish you could stay longer."

"I'll stay in that cave for a few hours. Lead me to it." Luke stood up, and Lucy walked beside him toward the cave.

"We'll have to cover it carefully," Lucy warned. "My folks are so strict about covering that cave, you wouldn't believe it."

"Yes, I would. Your pa's about the only person here in the States who's been good to me, but I can see he's strict, too. That's why if you told him about me being here, he wouldn't like it." Luke looked down at Lucy. "I don't know if I can trust you not to tell anyone while I'm down in this hole in the ground. But then—" and he shrugged his shoulders, "I don't have much choice. You know all about me now, and I've got to rest until dark."

Topsy was jumping beside them, and suddenly she stood up and walked three or four hind-leg steps beside Luke. "Jiminy, that's a smart dog," Luke said. "Trick dog, isn't she? Look, do you think you could carry a message for me? You going to the county fair in Langdon?" And when Lucy nodded, Luke went on.

"My best friend from Pilot Mound trains dogs— sounds silly, but he's real good at it. He'll be at the dog sideshow at the fair. Name's Toby Shaw. Got it? Toby Shaw. You find him and tell him I've gone ahead of him. We're enlisting in the army."

"Luke!" Lucy was alarmed. "People get killed in armies nowadays." Then she saw it was the message to Toby that was important to Luke. Armies he knew about. "Trust me, Luke. I've run errands for our family ever since I could walk."

At the cave, Luke easily lifted the heavy top, went down a couple of steps on the ladder, then reached up with both hands, and while Lucy guided it, he moved the cover into place.

"Dark enough in here," he said. "Now you and your pooch go away, and I'll snooze. Call me when it gets dark, if you can."

Lucy put her face close to the cover. "Luke, won't you get hungry tonight on the road home?" Lucy murmured. "I've read that men crossing a desert carry dried dates. Want some?"

"Bright girl! Run get them before I fall asleep," Luke answered.

As Lucy ran again toward the house, she told herself, "I mustn't leave a stone unturned." So she picked up not only the packages of dried fruit from Mother's shelves, but also the forty-five cents from her little red purse, all the nickels she'd saved to spend on the trip to Minneapolis.

When she handed everything down to Luke, she said, "Here's your desert food, and this is all the money I've got. You might need it." Luke took everything she handed him, but he didn't say thank-you. Perhaps an escaped prisoner sometimes forgot his manners.

Lucy washed the dishes at the pump. Then she returned to the stone house and sat gently rocking in her little chair, looking as though she'd spent all afternoon reading an adventure story instead of living one.

Father came home for supper about six o'clock and suggested they eat out on the porch. So Lucy dished up a big helping of beans for him and a very small one for herself. The brown bread she also put on a plate in the kitchen. But the pie was a problem.

"Bring the pie out here," Father said. "Then we can each have as much as we like." When she brought it out and half of it was gone, he looked at her sharply. "For heaven's sake! Did your mother bake only half a pie, or did Topsy get into it?"

"I was hungry," Lucy explained.

"Hungry enough to eat half a pie?" Father asked. "I don't believe it." For a moment Lucy thought she had been caught in her fib, but he was only surprised.

"I really don't want a piece now," Lucy told him, though she would have loved some of it. If she ate any, there wouldn't be a smidge left, and Mother would suspect something, even if Father didn't.

After supper they walked up and down the rows of vegetables in the garden, although Lucy was thinking much more of Luke hiding in the cave than of cucumber vines and potato bugs.

When Father pulled a fat red radish to munch on, Lucy pulled one too, though ordinarily she spurned radishes. "Lucky you didn't go to the Ladies Aid. You'd have disgraced us with your big appetite," he joked. And while he laughed, she pulled up a second radish and rapidly chewed that one down to its leaves also.

Later, when Father lay on the sofa dozing, she waited until he was snoring and the kitchen clock said nine o'clock. Then taking Topsy in her arms to keep her quiet, Lucy tiptoed out the back door and hurried to the cave.

Through one big crack between the boards, she could look down, but it was too dark to see anything. "Luke," she whispered in a faint whisper. "Luke, you awake?" No answer. So she spoke a little louder. "Luke, you said to call you." Still no answer.

But Topsy could tell someone was breathing down there, and she began to paw the boards and whine. Probably it was Topsy's scratching that wakened Luke, for almost at once he said, "Yes? Who is it?"

Before Lucy could answer, Topsy whined again and Luke whispered fiercely, "Go away, little beast!" Then he remembered Lucy. "And I don't mean you, little girl. Got the time?"

"It's just about nine," Lucy said. "And when my mother gets home, I can't come out again. And Luke, it's going to rain. Whatever will you do if it rains?"

"Get wet, I suppose," Luke whispered back. "But I won't shrink. And if it really pours, I don't want to drown in your brother's cave, so I'll move to your club-house until it's pitch dark and I can set out. Okay with you?"

"Nobody looks into the stone house at night," Lucy said. Then she heard an auto, and she began to panic. "My mother's home and my father will wake up and I've got to go in. And Luke, how will I ever know what happens to you?"

"Don't you worry, little girl," Luke whispered comfortingly. "Soon I'll slip into your snug little house. And by midnight I'll be almost to the border." He slightly pushed aside the cover and stuck his hand through the small open space.

"Shake on it, Lucy. I'll get there," he said. "And someday you can tell your folks—but not till you hear I'm in the army. And thanks. I don't know what I'd have done if you hadn't been here."

Lucy shook the hand he reached up to her. And at that moment, Mother called from the back door. "I'm home now, dear. It's starting to rain. Come along in."

As Luke moved the cover back across the cave and the rain began, Lucy whispered as loud as she dared, "Good-bye, Luke, and good luck!" Once in the house, she was safe and dry. But poor Luke wasn't safe, and pretty soon he wouldn't be dry either.

After she had gone to bed and to sleep, she wakened to hear Father coming up the stairs. "Father," she called to him, "what's wrong? Anything happen?"

"No, no, go back to sleep," Father soothed her. "I thought the barn door was banging, but when I went out I found it was the stone house door. I put the peg through the hasp, so now that's locked tight and your things won't get wet."

The stone house door locked on the outside? Lucy's

heart stopped for a second. What if Luke was locked in? In the morning he'd be found and taken back to jail. Should she try to sneak out and unlock it? But of course she'd be caught.

"What time is it, Father?" she asked.

"Soon be dawn—almost morning," he answered.

So if Luke was lucky, he was already across the border, home again in Canada. Lucy turned over to sleep some more.

When morning came and it was truly light, Lucy dressed and went quietly down the stairs. In the kitchen she roused Topsy for an excuse to go out so early. Topsy was not at all enthusiastic about either the early wakening or the cold wet grass, but she ran obediently with Lucy to the clubhouse.

Swiftly Lucy jerked the peg from the metal hasp and swung open the door. Inside, the stone house was empty.

The Chautauqua
Comes to Town

Amory was late coming home from the Schneiders'
farm, so the family sat down to Sunday dinner without
him. Usually on summer Sundays, they drove across the
border for a picnic on the Pembina River in Canada,
but that day the roads were muddy and Father was
happier with the auto in the barn instead of in a ditch.

"I've got this new geology book, so if we can't go
to the Pembina today, let's learn more about it," Father
began right after the blessing. "Did you know that little
stream was once a wide, wide river, and—"

Lucy cut in. "Does that book have anything about a
place called Pilot Mound? It's in Manitoba, too."

"Good question," Father replied. "I'll see," and he
shuffled through page after page, until Mother reminded
him of the dinner.

"Harry, couldn't you carve the roast? The gravy is about to become a glacier," Mother warned.

"Well, I must satisfy your mother's awful appetite, but I do know that mound was long ago a signal hill for the Indians," Father continued as he carved the roast. "Lucy, if you'll just reach me that dark green book on the lowest shelf—it's all about the Plains Indians."

Lucy didn't reach for the book, only asked another question. "But it's the town of Pilot Mound I'm really interested in. What do you know about the town?"

"Not a blamed thing," Father admitted almost crossly. "I don't have a single book on Manitoba towns. But let me see—" he rubbed his chin thoughtfully, "recently I've heard of someone from there. Oh, yes. That's where Luke Morgan came from." As he passed Mother her plate, he said, "Caroline, did I tell you the county sheriff's looking for Luke? He escaped from jail, just disappeared. No one knows where."

"Gone to Canada," Lucy said before she thought. Then she tried to patch up her mistake. "I mean, wouldn't it be likely? That's what I'd do if I escaped from jail."

"Gracious, Lucy, you're not planning how you'd escape from jail, are you?" Mother laughed. "Still dreaming of last year's Chautauqua play?" Then Mother began to speak to Father. "At the Ladies Aid yesterday, Mrs. Cochran said Luke never should have been jailed at all. But Mr. Owen said the young man was in the blind pig so he deserved what he got." While Mother talked she unclipped and clipped her pince-nez glasses on the bridge of her nose. This was always a sign that Mother was very impatient with someone, and it must be Mr. Owen.

"In the meeting after that, while Mr. Owen told about

those Eskimo missions, I felt more sorry for Luke Morgan than for those Canadian Eskimos. Bad of me, wasn't it?"

Amory and Jerry came in before Father could reply. "Met Jerry on the way. Could we have dessert together, before he goes home to dinner? Some pie, maybe?" suggested Amory.

"Funny thing about that pie, Caroline," Father said. "At supper it was already half gone. And your Lucy with that tiny stomach of hers had eaten as much as Amory ever has."

"Why didn't you help yourself to beans instead, Lucy?" Mother asked. "Much better for you than so much pie at one gulp."

"But you can't eat more than a certain amount of beans at one time," Lucy quoted Luke. Then she decided to clear the whole food problem at once. "That brown bread looked so good that most of that's eaten too, along with a big chunk of butter." Lucy avoided saying that she had consumed all this, so it wasn't a real lie.

"Lucy Johnston!" Mother exclaimed. "You may grow to full size after all. Tonight I'll cook extra liver for you and make a larger dish of bread pudding, too."

So Lucy saw that she'd be stuffing herself for days on food that she didn't like to save Luke and to hide her own fibs.

"Better check your cave, Amory, after last night's downpour," Father said.

After the boys went out, Lucy sat tensely, afraid Luke might have changed something in the cave. But soon the boys were back, with very muddy feet and only a worried question from Jerry.

"My father's going to have a fit, Mrs. Johnston. I

borrowed his jackknife to use in the cave and I didn't ask him first, and now it's not there." Poor Jerry looked very upset.

"The cave's been covered the whole time, Jerry," Mother answered. "Just ask Lucy."

Luckily, no one did ask Lucy, for she could guess where the knife was—in Luke Morgan's pocket. He needed it more than Jerry's father, but she couldn't tell that to anyone.

On Monday morning, the Owens were all well, so the Stone Age Girls held a business meeting in their clubhouse, which turned out to be mostly a discussion of the circus. In midmorning Mother called Lucy indoors. "Come in and use your eyes for me, Lucy," she said. "I want to make filled cookies, and I can't find a single date or dried apricot on the shelf."

So Lucy pretended to search. She pushed the boxes around, and she peered behind the taller jars, and all the time she felt as guilty as a thief.

"Never mind," Mother said after a few minutes. "I must have used them the last time I baked, unless you ate them on that eating spree you had last Saturday." Mother laughed. "You didn't eat those too, did you?"

Lucy could honestly answer, "Of course I didn't eat them. How big a pig do you think I am?" But as she hurried back out to the girls she wondered if she'd ever be free of Luke's demanding appetite.

At supper Father explained that the Chautauqua would be in Wales for only one day, Thursday. "This summer they tried hauling the tent and equipment from town to town by truck," Father said. "But they had breakdowns so often that they're using the trains again. The tent comes on the early morning freight, and after the afternoon and evening programs, everything goes back down the line."

"I'll bet we just get a dumb lecture and a bunch of singers cat-er-wauling up on the platform," Amory grumbled. "And if they have another smooching kiss like last year, I'll make that smack on my arm so loud that—"

Mother interrupted him. "Can't you wait until we see what the program is before you begin plans to spoil it?"

"And don't forget, Amory," Father cautioned him, "I'm putting up some of the money to bring this Chautauqua here. If you behave like a clown and make their programs seem funny, I'll stop your allowance for a month."

"Okay, but they'd just better not—" Amory noticed Father's scowl, and he shut up.

To change the table conversation, Mother asked Amory, "Have you thought what we might give you for your birthday that will be easy to carry? We'll be on our trip then, neither here nor there."

"All I want is cold hard cash," Amory announced.

"But I haven't any cash to give you," Lucy told him.

"No cash?" he said. "You've been hoarding nickels for weeks."

"Honest," Lucy answered soberly, "every nickel's gone."

"Why Lucy Johnston, what a spendthrift," Mother scolded.

"I didn't spend them." And before she realized it, Lucy added, "I gave them away."

"Well, well," Father said, "Canadian missions, I suppose. A donation to one of those affairs Mr. Owen is so tied up in?"

"Sort of," Lucy answered, hoping that would end it.

And before any more questions were asked, Mother apologized. "What a good girl. I'm glad you didn't just spend them."

On Thursday morning, after the freight train had been unloaded, Lucy and the four Owens went to Main Street, and standing at a safe distance, they gazed at the big canvas top slowly rising to yells and grunts and warnings of the Chautauqua crew, accompanied by loud advice from almost every man in town. Shortly before noon the tent was up, the ropes were tightened, the player piano from the school was hoisted onto the platform, and long rows of folding chairs were set up.

The four girls and Edward were about to leave for home, when a handsome curly-headed young crewman came over to them. "You girls want to earn a nickel apiece?" He gave them a warm smile. He was barely old enough to be called a man, but he wasn't a boy.

"We can't stay very long," Gwen answered.

"And I have to have a nickel, too," Edward insisted. "I'm their squire."

"What's that?" asked the man good-naturedly.

"I don't know, but I'm it," answered Edward.

"There'll be a nickel for you, but it's the girls I want to hire. Takes girls to dust chairs right. Here's four feather dusters, girls, and when every chair's clean as a whistle, you'll get your nickels and that squire of yours, too," he promised. He handed them the dusters and disappeared down the street into the poolhall.

The girls dusted and swished and dusted, and under the canvas tent the air grew hotter and hotter. By noon, they had dusted every chair, working as fast as they could. They had kept Edward, in his white suit, off in a corner, so he was still beautifully clean. But the girls were grimy and sweaty.

For a few minutes they sat just inside the open flap, waiting for the young man to return. Then Edward grew restless, and Gwin said, "Why don't I go and peek inside the poolhall?"

"You certainly will not go near that poolhall," Gwen said bossily.

"What's inside that poolhall?" asked Guinnie.

"Papa says it's a den of in-iq-uity, and that means it's full of sins. You can't imagine all that goes on in there," and Gwin rolled her eyes to look horrified. "It's worse than the blind pig!"

To stop Gwin from dragging out more of her papa's opinions, Lucy hastily offered, "All of you go on home, and I'll collect."

Off they went, and Lucy, left alone, stacked the four dusters and settled down on the end chair of the last row, where she could watch the street. Sitting there, she thought again that the Wales Main Street was nothing to brag about. She tried to imagine how it would look to strangers, to her city cousins, for instance—the raw boards of the new general store, the two holes where the drugstore and the hardware store were burned out last winter, the two dirty windows in the front of the poolhall, with sagging curtains pulled across them to keep the poolhall a secret place, and the street itself, rutted and dusty and empty.

Then the young man came out of the poolhall and strolled across to her. "Hello, little girl, can I do something for you?"

"Yes, you can pay us for all that dusting," Lucy answered.

"Us? What do you mean by *us?* I see only one of you," he said.

"I'm us, and you know I'm us." Lucy said it sharply,

trying to impress him.

"Do you know what I just did?" he said very pleasantly. "I forgot all about paying for that dusting, and I spent all my silver except for one dime. I really did." And he smiled again.

Lucy drew herself up as tall as she could. "Mr. Chautauqua, do you mean you're not going to pay us?" She frowned at him. "Are you some kind of city slicker? Do you think you can fool us just because we live in a little village like Wales?" And she glared at him.

He had turned to go into the tent, but now he came back to her. "You take this dime, and this afternoon, right after the program, I'll be standing here with the fifteen cents for the others. You'll trust me, won't you?" He gave her his broadest smile and patted her on the shoulder.

As Lucy hurried home, she was a little ashamed about all this pother for some nickels. But she'd also learned something. That young man had a nice smile, but it was just a smile he used to get what he wanted. It didn't mean a thing.

The afternoon was hot, and under the tent it was blistering, almost boiling hot. But women and children filled several rows of seats. Some people had even driven down from Hannah, the next town, which was the last one on the railroad branch line. Perhaps because Hannah people were strangers, they always looked more citified than Wales people. Lucy knew all the Wales people, of course. And to her surprise even Amory had finally decided to come. He and the other two Cave Men sat in the front row to spy on the magician.

When it was past three o'clock a tall elderly man with drooping shoulders under a drooping black coat walked onto the platform and stood behind the pulpit, near the player piano.

"First I shall recite some scenes from *Romeo and Juliet*, the tragedy of those two young lovers who died for love," he began. At the words *lovers* and *love*, the Cave Men poked each other so hard in the ribs that Jerry let out a little squawk.

"To set the right mood," the lecturer continued, "I wonder if someone in the audience would come up here and play a few bars of sad music. Is there a volunteer?"

Mother waited a moment and then went up the three steps to the piano on the platform, as everyone expected her to. Lucy saw that a player roll was attached in the front of the piano, but thought surely Mother could see that also. Then as Mother put her feet on the pedals and her fingers on the keys, ready to play sad, sad music, she must have touched the switch that began the player.

The keys flashed up and down without Mother's touching them, Mother reared back as though she had been attacked, and the player piano played the opening bars of "The Star-Spangled Banner." Everyone looked at everyone else to see what to do, but soon everyone was standing up and beginning to sing, "Oh, say can you see." Lucy was so embarrassed that she wanted to hide her head. What would those Hannah folks think of Mother? But with great aplomb, Mother kept pedaling to the end of the song. When the national anthem came to a stop, Mr. Owen came up to push the switch to *off*. But Lucy wondered whether Mr. Owen, who tumbled into a cave on top of his children, could be trusted to fix a mechanical piano.

The lecturer read several scenes from *Romeo and Juliet*, without a try for more music. The whole time the front row of Cave Men kept poking each other black and blue. Then the speaker announced his next

play was *Hamlet*. Perhaps to give Mother a second chance, he again invited her to the piano. "Let's have just a few bars, solemn and sad, for this tragic Prince Hamlet," he said.

This time Mother should have been wary, but she was so sure that Mr. Owen had switched off the roll that she put her foot on the pedal, her fingers on the keys, and went right ahead—right ahead into "Yankee Doodle Dandy." The audience gasped and then giggled. Immediately Mother shoved in the player switch, held it tight with her right hand, and with her left hand she played a funeral march, very bass and rumbling. If you could forget her opening of "Yankee Doodle Dandy," Mother's performance this time was very fitting.

The last reading was from *Macbeth*. Lucy hoped Mother would stay put, but when the lecturer gestured, Mother was again at the keyboard. Lucy sat breathless. She hadn't been in the Wales school all those years without knowing what came next on that roll.

Mother this time tested the switch, but she didn't hold it in. She simply launched into what she considered the proper music for all those royal murders. Foot on the pedal, hands on the keys, Mother began, or rather the player piano began, "Old Macdonald Had a Farm." And Mother was so shocked that for a moment she shut her eyes and kept on pedaling.

The Cave Men began shouting the song at the top of their lungs, the other children scattered around the tent took up the song, and Mother, who was laughing now, stopped pedaling, but she waited until Old Macdonald's donkey brayed its last hee-haw, before she again tightly held the switch at *off* and played a one-handed royal march.

Then Mother stood up, apologized to the lecturer and

to the audience, and came back to her seat beside Lucy. For once in her life, Lucy wished Mother wasn't her mother, wasn't even anyone she'd ever seen before. She wondered if things like this happened anywhere but in Wales.

With all the extra music, not much time remained on the program for the magician. Just before he began, Mother moved to the Cave Men's front row to guarantee good behavior, so Lucy moved with her.

Unfortunately this magician specialized in the simple tricks that Amory already knew from his book on magic. So when the man did a card trick that he was sure no one in this audience of women and children could solve, he asked in his smooth way, "Anyone care to come up and show me how this is done?" And leaning almost into the front row, he added, "I'll give a dollar to anyone who can figure it out." To Amory this was bait.

He jumped to his feet—and so did Mother. He started toward the platform, and Mother started too. In an instant he was almost beyond her reach, but she was able to snatch at the seat of his pants. Amory tugged forward. Mother pulled back. And the seam of his old knickerbockers gave way with a loud rip, so loud that it could be heard all over the tent.

Amory sat down, and so did Mother. By that time Lucy was so exhausted by her family's publicity that she sank back in her seat and wished she were invisible. What would the Chautauqua people think of them and their town?

When the program was over, Amory ran for a side exit; and Mother, with Lucy trailing behind her, greeted everyone as they went out. She said, "Hello," and "How do you do?" and "Wasn't the player piano awful?" She seemed not at all upset by the shameful goings-on, even before the Hannah folks.

As they left the tent, Lucy kept her eyes open for the Chautauqua man, but he was nowhere in sight. And remembering his slick manners, Lucy was not surprised. The one dime she would have to give to Guinnie and Edward, even though Edward hadn't done a mite of work, only stayed clean. In her mind being cheated rather evened up the afternoon's disasters. Chautauqua people were no better than Wales people, maybe.

At supper Amory reported that Mother had cheated him out of a dollar and ripped his pants off him in public. And before Mother could tell her side of the story, he told about her piano pieces and ended with, "Talk about making those programs seem funny! Why I couldn't do all that Mother did even if I tried. I'm never going to the Chautauqua with her again."

Mother finally got in a few words. "I didn't think it was fair for Amory to embarrass that magician in front of all those people."

Father agreed, but he added, "Sounds to me as though the Johnstons were already part of the show. That was an unusual choice of music, Caroline."

"Choice!" Mother laughed. "I've learned that with a player piano there is no choice. I vow I'll never again try to outwit a mechanical piano."

That night the whole Chautauqua company was putting on the operetta "Pinafore." So after supper, Mother played some of the songs on their own piano, which was not a player piano, and Father sang them out very, very loudly. Then he explained the story was about two babies switched by a nurse.

"Well, of all the bum ideas for a play," Amory said scornfully. "Can you imagine someone mixing up babies?"

"But Amory, look how different our red hair is from all our cousins," Lucy said. "Didn't you ever think we might be from a different—"

Amory wouldn't let her finish. "You dumb dumb-bell!" he hooted.

And Mother said, "Lucy, you read too many stories. And whenever you hear of escaped prisoners or switched babies you always think it could happen to you."

That night the tent was packed. Everybody in the country drove into town, and everybody living in town was there, too. As the chorus came forward for the first song, Lucy recognized the young Chautauqua man, singing and dancing and smiling. She knew he'd never pay those nickels, but he was very handsome in his bright blue uniform; she knew that too—and so, obviously, did he.

To Lucy the singing and the flounced dresses and the brass-buttoned naval uniforms and the dancing and the happily-ever-after ending were far more magical than anything the magician had tried. And when the last note and the last bow were over and the crowd went slowly out into the cool night, Lucy felt as though she were in a city, leaving a really truly theater.

When Wales had a night of Chautauqua, it was as exciting as Minneapolis must be—or perhaps even Chicago or New York City.

Going to the Fair

On Friday it began to rain, and it rained for the next four days. The clubhouse was so damp and chill that the girls moved upstairs to Lucy's bedroom, where they created more and more elaborate dolls' dresses, copied from Mother's *Ladies' Home Journal*.

Father lifted the suitcases and satchels down from the barn loft, and Mother spent hours with a suitcase open in every room, as she tried to fit everybody's clothes into the smallest possible space for the journey.

Outdoors was so wet and so muddy that Lucy began to fear she'd lost the county fair as she'd earlier lost the circus. With the roads churned to sticky gumbo, Father would never try those twenty miles to Langdon for a fair. But on Tuesday morning the rain stopped, and one day of hot July sun made the roads passable again.

Tuesday evening, Mr. Dickerman knocked at the back door, and when both Father and Lucy went out, he asked, "Got any room to take Hilda and the twins along with you tomorrow? I heard you folks were going, and their cousins from Dresden are, too. So if you can get my kids in your auto, they could see the fair and go home with their cousins." He was a tall, thin man who looked tired around the eyes.

"Sure enough! We'll squeeze them in somehow, Pete. They need the fun of a fair," Father said.

"And how's Mrs. Dickerman?" asked Mother, who was now at the door.

"She's up and doing a day's work. That baby keeps her so busy—well, she's got no time for thinking, like she did after Peter—" Mr. Dickerman paused. "Anyway, it's Hilda feels it bad this time. Her baby he was, little Karlie—" and he turned away from the door, saying over his shoulder as he left, "What time you want the kids here in the morning?"

"Seven-thirty to eight," answered Father. "Glad we can take them."

So the pileup of children in the backseat next morning was almost suffocating, even with the top down. But everybody who went to the fair piled people in, whether they drove an auto or a buggy or a wagon. The Owens were going with the Quimbys—five Owens and two Quimbys—so their Ford, like the Regal, would have seven people jammed into it.

The Johnstons had gone only a couple of miles when they had to pass a horse and buggy ahead of them. Amory asked Father, "Want me to yell?"

"Yell? What in the mischief for? You yell at a horse and buggy on this road, and I'll leave the others in Langdon and take you right home with your mother and me. Is that clear?" Father sounded furious, and he used his loudest voice.

Lucy turned to Hilda and the twins and saw their eyes were almost popping out in fright. But Amory, of course, had an excuse. "I thought yelling at horses was okay." Father began to rumble at him, but Amory paid no attention. "I've been reading that guidebook for the trip, and I can show you where it says, 'It is considered advisable to use the voice when passing horses.' Honest! So I was just going to use my voice."

Father didn't answer, only drove faster. But Mother said, "I can't believe the author had ever heard your voice, Amory." Then she asked Father, "Must you race along at twenty miles an hour?" Mother was holding on to her hat and clutching the door of the auto as it jounced from rut to rut. "At this speed you're likely to lose a child or two."

The day was already hot, and Lucy suspected Father was speeding so he'd soon get out of the packed auto. Amory shouted, "Yippee! Are we speeding!" Hilda and the twins only clung to each other. They were used to a horse, and a horse at this speed would be a runaway.

Before nine o'clock, the Regal was crossing the tracks near Uncle Charlie Johnston's house. Father slowed down to drive along the street and stopped in front of the rambling house. Aunt Effie called from an upstairs window, "Come on in, all of you. I've got a second breakfast ready. Going to be a scorcher of a day, isn't it?" And she disappeared inside.

At the front door was Cousin Gen. She had beautiful dark wavy hair, big brown eyes like her mother's, and was already in college. She held the screen door wide open and called out as loudly as her mother. "Come on in out of the sun! Why didn't you have the top up to shade you, Aunt Caroline?"

"Wonderful prairie air today," Father bellowed. All Mother could have said was that she was never offered the choice of a top up. Father believed in fresh air.

Amory climbed over the backseat pileup and was first at the front door. "Is the Ferris wheel as high as last year? What time does the airplane go up? Has Ed won anything at the booths yet? And I'm so hungry—got any of your good doughnuts, Aunt Effie?" Then without waiting for any answers, he went into the house.

For both Amory and Lucy, their cousins' house was like a second home. It was bigger than the Wales house, built for a bigger family, but still a house that they both knew from the dark cellar with the forever pumping pump to the odd upstairs bedroom that seemed built by accident, since there was no way into it except through other bedrooms.

Lucy and Hilda untangled themselves from the twins' legs, and though Lucy's long white stockings were smudged by little boys' heels, she was so glad to unfold herself that she didn't mind. Taking a twin by each hand and with Hilda coming along behind, Lucy ran up the front steps, kissed Cousin Gen and presented the Dickermans at the same time.

"You must be Pete Dickerman's children," said Aunt Effie, as they went in. "I'll bet you know Langdon from when you lived on the farm. Bought your groceries here, didn't you?" She was trying to make them feel at home.

"Yes, ma'am," Hilda answered, "but my ma won't come here anymore. She says our Peter caught infantile here last summer."

"Couldn't have been here. Wasn't a case in town,"

said Aunt Effie abruptly. Then she must have remembered their Peter had died and another baby boy had died since then. So she spoke very gently, "Well, you never know where those germs are, do you? Every summer, infantile is all over the state, and nobody can do anything about it."

"Second breakfast's on the table," called Gen, and they all moved toward the dining room.

There Uncle Charlie welcomed them. "Lo and behold! What do I see? Five children raring to go to the fair!" Then to Father he said, "Rain's been good for the crops, hasn't it? And George hired a truck and driver today to pick up scrap, so he'll get that junk in your yard, he says. Better hurry home, or he'll have your stove lids, too." He laughed then, his big hearty laugh.

"Where's Ed?" Amory asked, his voice louder than usual. Everyone had to speak louder in that house in order to be heard.

"At the fair," Uncle Charlie said. "He's yelling in front of Melchers' shed of farm machinery. Nobody paid much attention to it the first day, but now Ed barks 'It's free! Go on in!' and people probably go in to escape Ed's noise."

"Speaking of escape," Father began, "does anyone at the courthouse know what happened to Luke Morgan? You know, the young man arrested in the Wales blind pig."

"Since they never caught him, they think he crossed the border," Uncle Charlie answered. "But it's a long walk from here to the Canadian line. Funny, there wasn't a soul that saw him. Or if somebody did, they're certainly keeping it quiet."

At the cousins' house, they always teased Lucy about being quiet as a mouse, and right now she was glad. She sat eating doughnuts and drinking cocoa as though she'd never heard of a man named Luke Morgan.

And when she'd finished her second doughnut, she still said nothing, only looked around the big room, so different from the crowded, book-filled dining room at home. This dining room had white paneling and a wide mirror at one end that magnified the people, the table, and even the food, though there was always so much food that it didn't need magnifying.

"Is Len at the fair, too?" asked Lucy. "He told me he had a secret chemical formula that would win a prize. It wasn't a stink bomb, was it?"

Aunt Effie and Gen laughed so hard that all Lucy could make out of their answer was that Len had won a first prize for something—sounded like something chocolate.

"A cash prize? for what?" Amory was interested.

"For his chocolate fudge!" Aunt Effie repeated, still laughing.

Then Gen explained seriously. "Len's right, of course. Recipes are chemical formulas, and when boys can be chemists, why can't they be cooks? His fudge was so much better than any other batch there that everyone wanted the recipe."

"So last night," continued Uncle Charlie, "Len typed off a heap of copies, and he's selling them for a nickel apiece, to earn money to buy a bigger chemistry set."

"This family will be rich yet," Father said, laughing. "But where's Kink?" The oldest of the cousins, studying to be an electrical engineer, was named Kinsell, but everyone called him Kink.

"We haven't seen him for two days," Aunt Effie said. "He's tinkering with the wiring in that airplane on the fairgrounds."

"And Kink would rather be electrocuted than earn money, so he's working for nothing," Gen added. "But he's doing what he wants to do," she paused, "and he always did just that."

By now Amory had finished his fourth doughnut and was making plans. "Better get going, hadn't we? Any horse races today? Any fireworks tonight? Any new sideshows? And do you think Ed and I—"

Father now began talking at the same time. "Here's fifty cents for each of you and twenty-five apiece for the Dickermans, all in nickels, fresh from the bank." He handed Amory his share last. "That's all you get, Amory, so don't lose it, and don't borrow from Ed or Len, and don't—"

"Yeah, I know—and don't steal any either," Amory finished Father's sentence for him. "But if I win something that I can sell, then that money's mine, isn't it? And if I add that to the fifty cents, I'll have—" Amory went on talking, but no one listened, as they moved toward the front door. Father had to go back to the bank at once.

So Father and Mother kissed Lucy, gave Amory a final warning about money, and Mother got into the front seat while Father cranked and cranked. Eventually the engine began wheezing and chunking and then roaring. Father jumped in, and as they started off, he called, "We'll be back for you tonight. Have a good day at the fair!"

Immediately, Aunt Effie, who was the planner in their family, shooed everybody out to the Hudson, which was parked at the side of the house. "Now, Charlie, drive Gen and this pack of youngsters out to the fairgrounds," she ordered. "Gen's going to look after Lucy and the Dickermans for the rest of the morning. Amory won't be any help to them. He'll be off on his own affairs, won't you, Amory?" Aunt Effie knew boys, as a mother of four certainly should.

As they drew near the fairgrounds, the high Ferris wheel turning slowly in the sky, the tinny sound of the merry-go-round, the autos and buggies and people crowding through the wide gate—all of it was exciting to Lucy and just what she'd dreamed about. But it also made her feel rather afraid.

Then, going through the gate, she looked up at Gen, who must have understood, because she said, "When you've been in Wales all winter and spring this takes a bit of getting used to, doesn't it, Lucy?" And as she put her arm around her, she asked, "How long have you been waiting for this fair?"

"Almost forever." Lucy grinned. "Sometimes absolutely everything away from Wales seems marvelous to me."

"Ma and Pa brought me to the fair two summers ago," Hilda broke in. "The twins stayed with Aunt Aggie, so they've never been before. This time we're all just lucky to—" Hilda stopped. Perhaps she's bashful about saying she's lucky when she's lost Karlie, thought Lucy.

"Hilda, since you are here again, and it's the first fair for the twins, let's have a specially good time," Gen said in a comforting way. "Now where shall we start?"

Adolph and Rudolph, for boys who had never been to a fair before, had very clear ideas on where to start. "The merry-go-round!" they shrieked in their united way. Then they shouted in such a bumble of sound that you couldn't tell who wanted what. "I want spun-sugar candy, like Hilda told us about." "I want a ride on the Ferris wheel." "I want a chocolate ice-cream cone." "I want a strawberry one." "I want to see—"

Gen interrupted. "First, the merry-go-round. That you agree on." And she led them directly to it, since you couldn't miss its round-and-round again tunes. But there they had to wait until the twins got identical gray prancers to ride. Lucy and Hilda, side by side, rode white swans.

After a couple of turns, with all the upping and downing, Lucy understood why Gen preferred standing at the side in spite of the dust and crowds of waiting people. But the twins could have spent the rest of the morning on their wooden horses, and Hilda looked happy with her swan. So Gen paid for the Dickermans to ride once more. This gave Lucy her chance to ask about a sideshow with trick dogs.

"I'm not that interested in dogs, Lucy," Gen said, "but I know you are. Once we get these children off this whirligig, we'll go along the midway, and you keep your eyes open for a picture of dogs in front of a sideshow. Are you sure there is one this year?" And she looked questioningly at Lucy.

"Oh, I'm sure." But she didn't add how she was sure. She just waited until the merry-go-round stopped and they could all move on.

Sideshows and Cheats

As the five of them walked along the broad lane between the booths where you shot at moving ducks or
threw a rubber ball at a clown's face or tossed rings
onto big hooks, they heard a shouted, "Wow—eee! I hit
the bull's-eye!"

It was Amory. He was standing with Ed at a counter
where you shot with small rifles at a black-and-white
bull's-eye target. Amory had just hit the bull's-eye, a
surprise even to Amory, and much more of a surprise
to the owner of the stand.

"Hey, you kid," said the wide stomachy man behind
the counter, as he moved to stand in front of the target
for a moment. "You couldn't do that! What's the idea,
saying you hit the bull's-eye. No boy's done that—
ever. Take a look," and he shifted away from the target.

Sure enough, there was no hole in the bull's-eye, but instead one on the outer edge of the target.

"I hit it! I know I did!" screamed Amory.

"He did! He did! We saw the hole right in the middle!" yelled Ed, loud enough to be heard half a mile away.

"You two—who are you?" sneered the fat man. "You're just a couple of smarty kids. Look where the hole is. That's no bull's-eye."

Amory's screams and Ed's yells had begun to draw a crowd, and through the crowd, Gen led Lucy and the three Dickermans. Gen was never afraid of anyone, fat man or thin man, so she spoke up at once. "One of these boys is my brother and one is my cousin, and they aren't the ones doing the cheating here. I want to look behind that target to see if there's someone there closing up holes and opening new ones. And if there's any cheating going on, I'll report you to Mr. Groom. He's in charge of this fair, and you'll lose your license."

For a moment no one said anything. The crowd was quiet, wanting to hear every word. Even Amory and Ed were quiet. Out of breath, Lucy decided. The fat man stood silent, too, glaring at Gen, with her collection of children around her.

Then he decided to bluster again, hoping to avoid giving Amory the enormous Kewpie doll that was first prize. "Look who's talking," he said harshly. "These boys ain't no relation to you. That red-haired boy don't look one bit like you. Now mosey along," and the man leaned over at Gen as rudely as he dared.

The crowd moved closer, and a young man forced his way to the front and jumped over the counter. He wasn't very big, and his tight suit was an odd green color, but to Lucy he looked like a real hero. "You better quit your game, old man," he shouted to the booth owner, "or I'll knock your block off!"

"Not until I've knocked yours off," threatened the fat booth man. He grabbed the slight young man by the collar and was about to push him back against the metal counter, when another young man, much bigger, much heavier, and dressed in greasy coveralls, came elbowing his way through the crowd and vaulted the counter. This man didn't say anything, just grabbed the fat man's arm and twisted it until he let go of the young man's collar and howled, "Let me go! Let me go!"

And everybody shouted, "Give it to him! Give it to him! He tried to cheat! He's a cheat!" Lucy was cowering behind Gen, but now she peered around and recognized the rescuer. It was Kink in his oily mechanic's coveralls.

When Kink had the whole story, he reached up to the shelf above the target and lifted down the biggest, most taffeta-skirted Kewpie doll there. It was all of two feet tall, and as was usual with Kewpie dolls, it had nothing on above its hips.

Kink handed it to Amory, saying, "Here, Amory, I don't know what you want the darned thing for, but you hit the bull's-eye so legally it's yours." Then to the booth owner, Kink said only one sentence. "From now on, whoever hits the bull's-eye gets a prize. Okay?"

Then Kink started back to the airplane, first winking at Lucy and laughing. "I hope you like Kewpie dolls more than I think Amory does," he said.

At almost the same instant, Amory thrust the gigantic doll into Lucy's arms. "Here, Lucy, you take care of it for the rest of the day."

"Oh, Amory, I don't want to hang onto that all day," Lucy objected.

"Well, do you think I do?" asked Amory, and he rushed off with Ed before she could return it to him.

"That's just like a man," Gen said. "You're stuck with something he didn't want. He only had to have it to prove he'd won."

Lucy stared down at the half-naked object in her arms. It made her think of Gwin's hula dancers. Why did anyone want one? And why would the man try to cheat just to keep it? Hula dancers, Chautauqua men who cheated you out of nickels, and sideshow men who cheated over Kewpie dolls. To say nothing of doctors who drank and men who kept blind pigs. For a moment it all seemed too much.

"Don't you love it, Lucy? It's so big and so beautiful," Hilda said, bringing Lucy back to the midway. "Sometimes maybe you and Amory could let me borrow it?" And Lucy nodded, because she couldn't think of the right answer.

"Where next?" asked Gen. "Any exhibits you'd like to see?"

"The strong man! The strong man! Yah, the strong man!" shouted one twin or the other or both.

"He's not an exhibit. He's a sideshow," said the all-knowing Hilda. "I'd like real well to see the patchwork quilts. Ma makes them, and when I go home I could tell her what was here," explained Hilda.

So they entered the barnlike building where home-crafts were on display. First-prize blue ribbons were stuck on everything from darned socks to chocolate cakes, from great round bunches of pink, rose, and lavender sweet peas to crocheted tablecloths and baby dresses. Up on the walls, like tapestries Lucy had seen in pictures of castles, hung the brilliant patchwork quilts. Hilda rattled off the name of every pattern—the sunburst, the crazy quilt, the flower garden, the hit-or-miss.

But a few quilts were enough for the twins. So Lucy followed them as they went swiftly out the farther door. "Hey, wait," a boy called to them. "Don't you know me?"

"It's the chemical boy!" the twins chorused, and Lucy knew that must be the name they used for Len.

"Sold all your recipes?" asked Gen as she and Hilda came out.

"All gone. Mrs. Gordon's bringing me some of her brown-sugar fudge to sample. After I get that, shall we go to tour the fair, Lucy?" Len asked.

"The Dickermans are meeting their Aunt Aggie by the grandstand. After that, I'll bring Lucy back here and you go with her, Len, to see everything we've missed," Gen said.

Off they went to admire the strong man's muscles, to buy cotton candy and ice-cream cones and Cracker Jack, and finally to ride on the Ferris wheel. Gen took a twin on each side of her, firmly buckled into the swinging seat. Lucy and Hilda climbed into another, Lucy clinging to Amory's Kewpie doll and Hilda clinging to Lucy.

Soon they were all lifted into the sky, far above the crowds and the noise and the town itself. When the wheel finally stopped to let someone off and someone else get on, Hilda and Lucy teetered and rocked at the top of the wheel, at the top of the world, and Hilda kept repeating, "Golly! Golly! Golly!" But Lucy only held her breath and wished they'd start the downswing so she could put her feet back on solid prairie. She preferred the view from the ground.

Try Your Skill

At noon, Gen shepherded them to the shady side of the grandstand. A stout woman with four small children called out, "Here we are! Had a good time, kids?" And their Aunt Aggie held out her arms to welcome the Dickermans. But as the twins began to clasp her, she jumped back, laughing. "We'll hug some other time. Right now you're too sticky." And for once, Lucy could tell Adolph from Rudolph, for Adolph was smeary brown from a chocolate cone and Rudolph was splashed in strawberry pink.

"Who won the doll?" Aunt Aggie's Clara asked in admiration. "Isn't she a dream?"

"Could we try for one?" begged Mamie, the littlest Dickerman cousin.

"They're awful hard to get," Hilda said. Which was certainly true, Lucy decided.

Then noticing how longingly Hilda was staring at the fat Kewpie and its ruffled taffeta skirt, Lucy suddenly saw a solution to her burden. "Hilda, would you like to have this doll to keep?" asked Lucy.

Hilda didn't wait for Lucy to change her mind. She simply put out her arms and carefully cradled the bull's-eye Kewpie. What Amory might say to this transfer of his property, Lucy couldn't guess. But she wasn't going to spend all of that broiling day lugging around a monster of a Kewpie doll.

Back at the exhibit shed, Len was waiting with a few pieces of brown-sugar fudge on a paper plate. "Good candy," he said as he stood up. "Want some?" And he continued eating it as they went along together.

"You'll spoil your appetite, Len," Gen said.

"Already spoiled," answered Len.

"Well, feed Lucy something at the next food stand. Then you two do anything you like until after the airplane goes up. That's the end of the afternoon program, and we hope it isn't the end of the plane," Gen said, quite seriously. "After that, Dad will be at the gate in the Hudson, and you come on home for supper. Have a good time, both of you," and Gen left.

"You hungry, Lucy?" asked Len.

"No!" Lucy answered emphatically. "I think we stopped to eat at every single stand on the fairgrounds."

"Okay. The sideshows then," said Len. "Any favorites?"

"I most want to see the trick dogs," Lucy said.

"We'll see them," promised Len. And the two of them set off along the midway between booths and counters and sideshow tents. They passed the tent for the fat woman, the thin man, the snake charmer, the two-headed calf, and the scarf dancers.

Near the tent of the fortune-teller they halted a moment. Dressed like a gypsy with gold hoop earrings and a scarf around her head, the fortune-teller sat on her platform looking for business. Lucy was tempted to spend the last of her money to know the future, but Len said, "Forget it! She'll say you're going on a journey to find happiness. Give me your cash, and I'll tell you that."

As they came close to the fortune-teller's tent, she turned her turbaned head toward Lucy and called out, "Come inside with me, little girl, and for half price I'll tell you about a journey you're going to take and how you'll find—"

Lucy and Len broke into a run, laughing so hard that they kept bumping into people. So they slowed down and stopped at each booth along the way to see what was there. But none of them seemed worth paying to go into.

At the far end of the midway, the worst place for a sideshow, was a small shabby tent with a battered platform in front of it. Over the entrance hung a faded canvas with a painting of five or six dogs doing tricks. Some were jumping through hoops, two were pushing dolls' carriages, and one was looking up at numbers on a blackboard, as though it could add.

On the platform stood a thin boy of twelve or so, and as soon as Lucy and Len came near, he began to yell, "Buy your tickets and come on in. See the fantastic, unbelievable dogs. Their tricks will amaze you. They can walk like people, they can count, they can almost talk. Get your tickets here. Just in time for the show!"

Then a grimy, scowling man stuck his head out the tent door and growled, "You shut your trap, Tom. Your ma and me ain't running a show for kids! Wait till there's a crowd." And he pulled his head back in.

Soon there was a hullabaloo of squabbling and screaming inside the tent. The boy jerked his head back toward the tent. "Ma and Pa at it again," and he shrugged his shoulders. "You giving that candy away?" He jumped off the platform and came up to Len.

"Want it?" Len handed him what was left on the plate, and it was gone in a jiffy.

Here was Lucy's chance to ask about Toby Shaw. "Does a man named Toby Shaw work for this show? I've got a message for him," Lucy began.

"Nope. Not now. Went back to the Bradna show in Barnum-Bailey." The boy used as few words as Len. "Know him? Ever seen the Bradna dogs?"

Lucy thought fast. If Toby Shaw was with the circus, how could she deliver Luke's message? She wanted to ask what Bradna dogs were, but instead she asked the boy, "Do you think I could write Toby Shaw at the circus? Would he get a letter?"

"Never." About that, the boy was very definite. "Circuses move around too much. But if you get a chance, see the thirty white Bradna dogs." He made it sound as fantastic as he had tried to make his cheap sideshow sound. "My pa used to work for that show. Now he boozes too much. But I know every dog and every trick, and all the white horses with them, too."

The fighting inside the tent had lulled, but now it started again. The boy jumped back on the platform, a cluster of women and children came down the midway toward them, and Lucy and Len turned back toward the grandstand. "Good-bye—and good luck!" Lucy called, but the boy was already off on his rigmarole, "Buy your tickets and come on in."

Lucy hadn't learned much about Toby Shaw, but she had seen something of sideshow life. It must be even more rough than life in Wales, and not really exciting— just hard.

"Kink's got a grandstand pass we can use," Len said. So they went to the far part of the fairgrounds, near the flimsy looking airplane, to get the pass. Lucy wondered how one pass was enough for two children, but Len settled that. "My cousin's so little that I got only one pass," Len said to the ticket collector and yanked Lucy in behind him.

The horse races and most of the cattle displays were over, and except for a few farmers, no one paid any attention to the final blue-ribbon cows and calves being led around the track. Everyone was talking about the airplane, how far it could fly, how long it could stay up, and how far up it went.

After a long wait, the airplane engine began to roar.

Then after another long wait, the airplane slowly lifted off the ground, looking like paper and matchwood sticks glued together. But it rose in the air, circled over the grandstand and then flew off to the south. And the crowd yelled, over and over again, "There she goes! There she goes!"

Lucy twisted her head far back as she watched it go out of sight. Up there, she thought, you must be able to see the whole county. A Ferris-wheel view was nothing at all.

When the plane wasn't even a speck in the sky, and the afternoon excitement was over, Lucy trudged behind Len through the ankle-deep dust as they pushed their way through the sweating mass of people. Near the main gate, across a stream of people going home, Lucy caught sight of the Quimbys and the Owens.

"Seen everything?" Lucy yelled to them.

"Absolutely everything," Gwin yelled back.

"Left no stone unturned!" Gwen shouted. Then the crowd shifted, and Lucy lost sight of them.

At the gate, Uncle Charlie was sitting patiently behind the wheel of the Hudson, and Amory and Ed were running up to the auto. When Lucy got to the auto, Amory was telling Uncle Charlie he'd stay for the night's fireworks.

"Tell my folks I'll come home on the train tomorrow, and this way they'll have more room in the Regal driving home, and so it's a really good—"

"I'll tell them," Uncle Charlie interrupted. "Just be sure you two come home together tonight."

And the two cousins ran back to the fair, while Lucy and Len climbed into the auto.

After supper, while it was still light but growing dusky, the folks drove up in the Regal. Lucy climbed into the backseat, and, the evening having turned cool, pulled the auto robe snugly around her and leaned back, half-asleep, while the folks stood chatting. Then Father cranked the auto, everyone waved and called, "Good-bye," and the Regal was turned toward home.

Lucy stayed cozily curled up so that she could watch the sky change and the prairie fade as dark came on. Drowsily, she half lay on the backseat, not listening to what Mother and Father were saying up front.

Then suddenly she sat up straight, for she heard Father say, "I'll go see him when we're in Minneapolis. He must want me back at the university."

"It's your chance to teach again, Harry. And we'd live in the city again." Mother spoke excitedly.

"The city's good for you, Caroline, but for me Wales—"

"Go to live in the city and leave Wales?" Lucy piped up from the backseat.

"We thought you were sound asleep," said Mother, looking around at Lucy. "But I suppose there's no harm."

"But I'm not sure I want to leave Wales and the Owens and my clubhouse," Lucy complained.

"Anyway keep your mouth shut about it," Father said. "And remember it's easier for Amory to keep a secret if he's never heard it."

So Lucy lay back again under the robe. And before she knew it, Father was shaking her gently and saying, "We're home. Wake up, so you can go back to sleep again."

He half lifted her onto her feet and helped her stagger into the house and up to bed.

Another Passenger

Lucy woke late the morning after the fair, saying to herself, "Three more days to wait! Three more days to wait!" It was a minute before she recalled what she was waiting for. Of course—on Sunday at five in the morning they were starting the four-day drive to Minneapolis.

Downstairs Mother was alone, ironing shirts, dresses, and petticoats for the trip. Since the breakfast table was cleared, she handed Lucy a tray with a shredded-wheat biscuit and milk and toast and peanut butter to take out to the stone house. Topsy now emerged from her box, stretching, yawning, and watching the contents of the tray.

The sun had already warmed the stone house, and Lucy sat at the small table with Topsy close at her feet.

Since there was no one else to talk to, she began talking to Topsy. "You should know, Topsy, that some dogs have a very rough life, much rougher than your life in Wales. For instance, in a sideshow—" But Topsy didn't want a sermon, only a bite of toast. So she sat up on her haunches and gave her sharpest bark.

"Yoo-hoo! Yoo-hoo!" It was the four Owens, Gwin as usual leading the pack and calling out, "We're going back to Canada!"

"Back to Canada!" Lucy at once saw herself waving good-bye forever to them at the depot. And her next thought was that she might as well move to the city after all.

As they drew near, Edward shouted, "Great-aunt Maud sent a train ticket for Mama, a big one, and a little one for me, too."

"And for me, too," squealed Guinnie. "I'm her little Maud Guinevere," Guinnie reminded Lucy.

By now they were all at the clubhouse, and Gwin was talking full-steam ahead. "And the other half-fare ticket's mine, because I'm the right age, and we leave next week, and—"

Lucy wasn't interested in Great-aunt Maud or half-fare tickets. "Are all of you going? And are you moving back there? And never coming back?" Lucy asked in a mournful voice.

"Of course, they're coming back," Gwen comforted her. "They'll only be gone a week or so, and Papa and I aren't going anyway." Gwen almost sighed, as she added, "I'm so old now that I'm full fare. So I'll stay home and weed the garden and cook for Papa and take care of Topsy for you the way Gwin was going to. Sometimes being the oldest is no fun at all," Gwen complained.

"Poor Gwen," said Gwin, and she probably did mean it, but she was so excited about her own trip that her voice was anything but sad. "And Lucy, Gwen did have an invitation to go to Fargo for a week to babysit for the Maclarens—those are people we used to know in Canada—but—"

"But Fargo is expensive to go to, if you're my age," Gwen finished the sentence. "It's really Moorhead they live in, across the river from Fargo—but if you can't get to Fargo, you can't cross the river!" Gwen was trying to be cheerful, but it was a feeble joke.

"Gwen! I wonder if my folks could squeeze you in. We're driving right through Fargo, and we'd pick you up on the way back, and—I'm going to ask! Can't leave a stone unturned!"

And Lucy continued to plan, almost as fast as Amory could. "Somebody else could keep my Topsy, and the weeds could grow in your garden, and your papa could learn to cook." Lucy stopped. Even she could see that part of the plan would never work.

The idea of Mr. Owen putting a pan right side up on the stove, let alone cooking something in it, was so fantastic that they all began to laugh.

"Papa getting a meal!" Gwen giggled.

"And eating what he'd cooked!" shouted Gwin.

"And cleaning up the kitchen afterward!" Guinnie shrieked. "Oh, that would be the best of all. Papa in the dishpan!"

"Well, not exactly inside the dishpan, Guinnie," Gwen said more seriously. "Anyway you see, Lucy, how much he needs me."

"I don't care how much he needs you, Gwen. If my folks have room for you, my mother can ask your folks, and maybe— We'll see," Lucy concluded.

Noon was the best time to ask about another passenger, before Amory was home to howl about taking one more girl. So Lucy began as soon as Father had said the blessing at dinner. "Do you think we could take Gwen with us—not all the way, only as far as Fargo?" Lucy began, and when she wasn't cut off, she hurried on.

"Mrs. Owen is taking the other three back to Canada to visit, and Gwen's too old for half-fare, and anyway they want her to stay home and cook for Mr. Owen."

"I don't see how we could, Lucy," Mother said. "It's such a long drive—500 miles, you know. We'll need every inch of space."

"And the more passengers, the more weight on the tires, my dear," Father added.

Lucy nearly burst into tears, but tears never got her anywhere, except sent off to her room. So she persevered. "But it's not all the 500 miles, only to Moorhead, where she can babysit for old friends. Besides, how would you like to stay home to cook for Mr. Owen, Mother?" And before Mother could say a word, Lucy turned to Father. "And how would you like to be alone with just Mr. Owen for all that time? Wouldn't that get your goat?"

"Lucy, that's very slangy," Mother said, though she grinned at Lucy's explosion.

"Mr. Owen is Gwen's father, not mine," Father argued. Then he laughed. "But you do make me feel sorry for her. I'll let your mother decide. She'll be in that crowded backseat, since Amory must ride in front to watch for trail signs and read the guide to me—something your mother's glasses don't adjust for."

Then he spoke directly to Mother. "What do you think, could three fit in that backseat for over 200 miles?"

Mother was slowly dishing up the dessert of floating-island pudding, each dish full of yellow custard with a mound of sugared meringue on top. Lucy watched, waiting for Mother's reply.

"As for taking Gwen," Mother finally said to Father, "you take Amory's friends with him every time you camp on the Pembina River, so why not Gwen for Lucy this once?" Then to Lucy she said, "I'll go right over to Owens' after dinner to ask, if you'll do the dishes."

Do the dishes! Lucy was willing to do a week's dishes if dishes would get Gwen into the Regal. Later, as Lucy dipped the warm water from the range reservoir into the dishpan, she overheard Mother saying, as the folks went out the shed together, "You have to remember, Harry, that the Owens may be in Wales only this one year, the way Methodist ministers move."

Then they were gone out the shed door, and Lucy felt a little sad as she washed the dishes in the soapy soft water. She had almost forgotten Mother's warning, even before the Owens came, that they might stay only a year. It seemed even worse now than it had then.

In half an hour, Mother was back, saying as she came in, "Gwendolyn can go with us, and this afternoon let's go down to the village and buy her a touring bonnet like ours. Don't you think she'd like that?"

"With the gray veil on yours and the blue one on mine, couldn't we get that pink one for Gwen? Oh, Mother!" Lucy could hardly believe her luck.

At suppertime, Amory came running in ahead of Father, telling all about the fireworks the night before. "Next Fourth of July, we've got to get displays like that for Wales," he insisted. "If you'll order something that shoots up like that and then spreads all over the sky in a flag or rainbows or whole towers of fire, I'll give you all my money, too. Right now, I'll give you what I'll get from selling that big doll I won at the fair. Where is it, Lucy?"

"I gave it to Hilda Dickerman," Lucy answered in a very small voice. Then she gained confidence, as she remembered Hilda's joy. "She wanted it so much, Amory, and you didn't even want to carry it and neither did I—and anyway poor Hilda needed a doll."

Amory recovered quickly from his shock. "You gave my first-prize Kewpie doll away? What kind of sister are you? Why I was going to sell that doll for ten dollars! That's what the booth man said it was worth." Amory was screaming at the top of his lungs. "You go right over to Dickermans' this minute and you get it back!"

"But I can't ask for it back! I can't!" Lucy was now screaming at Amory. "I gave it to her! She loves it! And anyway," Lucy turned to Mother, "do you think a Kewpie doll, even if it is about two feet tall, is worth ten dollars?"

"Doesn't seem likely," said Mother. Then to Amory she said, "Lucy can't go ask for something she's given away. It was nice of her to give it to a little girl who's had so much trouble."

"Nice!" yelled Amory. "Nice! Why it's the most dishonest thing I ever heard of. Here's Lucy giving away my ten dollars, and it's just like stealing from me, and you say it's nice!" Amory glared at Mother as fiercely as he had been glaring at Lucy.

Father roused himself from whatever he'd been thinking about. "Amory, that man in the booth was a thief. You know that. If he said that Kewpie was worth ten dollars, it probably was worth about fifty cents. Since you want a doll so much—"

"I don't want a doll! All I want is my money," Amory howled. "I was going to spend that money in Minneapolis on presents—presents for everybody." Amory said it in such a large way that you could almost see him passing out great armfuls of packages to all his friends. Amory really was generous, and sometimes did spend his money on someone else, if he could remember before he'd spent it on himself.

"All right," and Father took his billfold from his inside jacket pocket, "here's your pay. It's a one-dollar bill, and that's the last I want to hear about your doll, Amory."

"My doll!" Amory was about to continue the argument, but he dropped the subject and picked up the bill. "Next year, I'm going to win something like a big tea set, and I'll carry it home and sell it myself. Ed and I didn't win it, but we tried for one of those sets that the man said were worth twenty-five dollars." And Amory made it sound like twenty-five million.

Once Amory had rushed off to the cave to show his dollar to the Cave Men, Father pulled out a leather wallet and handed it to Lucy, saying, "It's empty, but it's brand new. That insurance adjuster gave it to me, and for once it doesn't have my name and his company's name printed on it. How about your giving it to Amory for his birthday present?"

"It is nice brown leather, but won't Amory want some of that cold, hard cash in it?" Lucy was doubtful about giving Amory an empty wallet that he might ask her to fill with her own money.

"I'll try to persuade him to hang on to that bill he just got," Mother said, but she didn't sound very sure. "At least it's easy to pack, Lucy, and Amory does like anything to do with money, even if there isn't any money in it."

"Trust Amory," Father chuckled. "He'll find cash to fill a billfold, even if it doesn't stay there very long."

The next afternoon, Mother sent Lucy to the flower garden to pick every single flower in bloom—sweet peas, asters, larkspur, white pearl, and mignonette. Together they made two huge bouquets. "Take one to Mrs. Bortz and the other to Mrs. Dickerman," Mother said. "Neither of them has a flower garden this summer. And hurry along, Lucy. We've still a lot to do."

Lucy went to Mrs. Bortz's back door, and there she was on the back stoop, shelling peas. "How good, how good," she said. "And flowers I need now, I surely do." She looked much more tired than the last time Lucy had seen her.

"Such bad news every day," Mrs. Bortz said, as she stood up to take the flowers in the house. "Such a terrible battle—such terrible killing—so many, so many dying." And when she saw that Lucy looked surprised, Mrs. Bortz asked, "You know about the battles? About every day more dead?" Then she tried to smile. "*Ach*, but you're young. Thank your ma, and take care on your long trip."

Lucy left her, and all the way to the Dickermans' she tried to remember what the headlines had said on Father's *Grand Forks Herald*. She did remember the big black letters BATTLE OF THE SOMME. Father had told them that was on the Western Front in France. But when she tried to imagine what war and battles and dying must be like, she gave up. It all happened in a different world from Wales.

At the Dickerman house, only Mrs. Dickerman was at home, and Baby Charlie, of course. Hilda and the twins were still at their Aunt Aggie's. Strangely enough, Lucy had never seen Mrs. Dickerman. She was darker than the others in the family, and she still looked sick, her straight hair pulled tightly back from her bony face.

"Thank your ma for the flowers," she said to Lucy. Then she began a long explanation of how she had to go to Main Street to buy yeast cakes and would Lucy sit a few minutes so Charlie wouldn't be left alone.

"Do you think Charlie's safe with only me?" asked Lucy. "My mother says he's a very delicate baby."

"You don't touch him, see? You just sit by his box so the cat don't jump on him. I come right back." And as she spoke, Mrs. Dickerman picked up a brown coin purse from the kitchen table, pointed to a rocking chair for Lucy to sit in, and went through the back door toward Main Street.

The kitchen was beautifully clean, the range was a shining black, and the board floor was scrubbed almost white. Lucy sat in the big wooden rocker near the two straight chairs that held Charlie's box, and she rocked silently to and fro, her feet touching the floor only as she rocked forward.

There was no clock in the kitchen, so Lucy had no idea how long she'd been rocking when she heard little stirrings and fussy noises in Charlie's box. Getting up, she peered into the box, and Charlie lay looking up at her in a blank way, like a little kitten when it first opens its eyes.

Then his mouth opened and he began to whimper, then to cry, and then to scream until he turned a bright red and finally a frightening maroon. He screamed and he screamed. Lucy went to the back door, but Mrs. Dickerman was not in sight. Back at the box, Lucy stood uncertainly. She'd been told not to touch him. But he looked as though he might explode at any moment.

"All I can do," Lucy said to herself, "is rock him, box and all." So she picked up the cotton-lined box. It was surprisingly light to hold an infant and his blankets. Going to the big rocker, she sat down gingerly and began to rock, making hushaby sounds. Charlie did close his mouth a bit, and she began to half sing to him.

"Funny sight I must be," she muttered to herself, "rocking a cardboard box. And yet—it's not so bad. A baby must be fun—that is if he isn't screaming, and if you don't have to put your arms around a box with sharp corners."

To and fro, to and fro, she rocked, and Charlie dozed off. Mrs. Dickerman finally came rushing in the door and then began to tiptoe, as she saw what Lucy was doing.

"Good girl," she said to Lucy under her breath. "First time I'm on Main Street. Everybody asking about Charlie and me." By now she had put her small brown bag of yeast cakes on the kitchen table and gently lifted the awkward box off Lucy's lap.

"Thank you and thank your ma," she whispered, as Lucy slipped out the door. "You're good with kids—I can see."

Topsy was delighted to see Lucy when she came home, but it took a few minutes for Topsy to seem important, after rocking a baby. Topsy had been a problem, since all the Owens were going to be away, but Jerry had offered to keep her, and Father was paying enough so that Jerry said he could buy a new jackknife for his father. Poor Jerry! Sometimes Lucy felt that Jerry was the only one paying the penalty for the blind pig and for Luke's escape.

Thinking of Luke reminded Lucy of Toby Shaw,

and she wondered whether there was any way she might get a message to him. The sideshow boy's "Never!" stuck in her mind, but after all she was going to the Barnum and Bailey Circus herself. Maybe there would be a way.

That evening Lucy repacked her clothes in a smaller suitcase, to make room for Gwen and for Gwen's satchel. It was while she was repacking that she saw, if she left home all the long black stockings but the one pair she'd wear, she could put in Clarissa's wardrobe and show the relatives her sewing.

And by leaving out the black buttoned shoes she also hated, she could put in Clarissa to model the wardrobe. None of the city cousins wore long black stockings and button shoes anyway. She'd look like a country cousin, for sure! Like a hick!

As she stuffed both the shoes and the stockings into the dark corner of her closet, she knew she should ask Mother about it. But she also knew exactly what Mother would say. So why ask and get a big "No!"

At supper the next night, the night before they were to leave, there was so much debate about whether the Regal could hold everything and everybody that Father began to tease. "Why don't we stay home, and Amory and I can camp for my vacation on the Pembina?"

But the night before a trip was no time to tease Mother. She looked so sourly at Father that he quickly changed his tone. "We're going, Caroline, and we'll get it all in, though I sometimes wish we were going in a covered wagon instead of the Regal."

"Covered wagon," Lucy said dreamily, "just like pioneers."

"Some pioneers!" snorted Amory. "Pushing off for the city to see the Biggest Show on Earth!"

The Long Journey
Begins

Since they were leaving so early in the morning, Gwen spent the night with Lucy. It wasn't pitch dark when they got up, but it was only dimly dawn. By lamplight they quickly washed and dressed and ate in the kitchen, standing up. Then they all packed themselves into the Regal, which was already so bulging, inside and outside, that it looked as though it had tried to swallow more than it could hold.

Lunch was in the big basket up front at Amory's feet. As soon as he got in, he lifted the cover to see what kinds of sandwiches there were, and then he forgot to put the cover down. Father cranked and cranked, and as the Regal began to stutter to a start, he yelled to Amory, "Quick! The spark lever!"

Amory jumped to obey, and both his feet landed in

the mound of wax-papered sandwiches. Amory screamed. Mother screamed almost as loud. "Watch—your—feet, Amory Johnston!"

By now Father was yelling again, "Amory, push up the spark! Up! Up as far as you can!"

Amory jerked the spark lever way up, but his feet went way down once more, bang scrunch on two dozen hard-boiled eggs.

This time Amory let out a long "Ooohhh!", and Mother only sighed and closed her eyes, as though she'd fainted. Lucy had pictured the deviled ham sandwiches squashed into the jam ones, and the chicken ones mashed with the chocolate cookies, but now she knew all over everything were cracked shells and flattened insides of hard-boiled eggs.

"Gee, I am sorry," Amory apologized. And as Father climbed in, Amory moved back to his place, holding his feet high in the air. "I'll eat what nobody else wants. Honest I will," he promised.

Mother didn't answer, but Father said cheerfully, "Never you mind, Caroline. Hash is the simplest form of food anyway."

After that, Mother wouldn't trust anyone to latch the big gate. But she was so tangled in suitcases, packages, and coats that she couldn't budge.

"Hey! Here comes Jerry," Amory shouted. "He's carrying Topsy. Probably couldn't stand that spoiled mutt more than one night."

Jerry ran up beside the auto, holding tight to Topsy. "Ran all the way! Just made it, didn't I? Topsy's fine. See?" He paused for breath. "Want me to close the big gate for you?"

Mother sank back in the seat. "Jerry," she said, "you may be a Cave Man, but sometimes you're a saint, too."

And Lucy said, "Thank you, Jerry, for bringing Topsy to say good-bye. And she's not even struggling to get out of your arms, is she?" Lucy didn't say this too happily, for who wants a pet completely happy with someone else in just a few hours?

Father backed out onto the road, and Jerry, still hugging Topsy, latched the big gate and waved. They were off. As long as they could see the house, Lucy and Gwen kneeled on the seat, looking back at Jerry waving, at Topsy in his arms, and then at the yellow house, and finally at the five tall cottonwoods with the rising sun glinting on their shiny leaves.

"Maybe some things in Wales are rough and wicked," Lucy said to herself, "but not my house and not our cottonwoods."

"Now we've got to get organized," Father began.

"Organized!" said Mother. "Just what do you think I've been doing for the last month?"

Father went right on. "Amory, open the guidebook to the marked page, and after we leave Langdon, you read aloud each direction and watch for trails on the barns, granaries, poles or even fenceposts. Remember we follow the color painted between the two white streaks, and the first one is red."

"And I'll keep a log of the trip in my little notebook, just to be sure," Mother said. "That guidebook is three years old, and you know sometimes the paint has faded or the fencepost is gone. Who knows," Mother continued, "we may need my logbook to get us home." Lucy had never thought of all this, and it sounded very grim.

Though Father said he was driving twenty miles an hour, it took them an hour and a half to go the twenty miles to Langdon, and another three and a half hours to go the fifty-five miles to Park River. "At this rate," Father teased, "we'll just about make Lake Minnetonka for one night with your family, Caroline, and then we'll have to start home."

"Harry, I don't like to complain," Mother said in a pained voice, "but there's something very uncomfortable under the two folded blankets on this seat. I can't imagine what it is, but it's more than a wrinkle."

"Oh, that's my BB gun," Amory said. "It was too long to put anywhere else, so—well, you remember that story about the princess who noticed a pea under all those mattresses? I knew nobody here was sensitive like a princess."

Mother finally got in a word. "Amory, I will not ride for four days on a BB gun, princess or not! You can just sit on it yourself."

"I couldn't," protested Amory. "I don't have enough behind to make it comfortable. Besides, it would be clear across this seat, and the driver shouldn't sit on a gun."

"Stop right here, Harry," Mother commanded. "This gun has to be strapped on the trunk-rack suitcases," and she dragged the BB gun out from under the blankets to hand to Father. With it gone, Lucy did notice the back-seat was considerably less bumpy.

As Father got back into the auto, he said, "Strapped safe and tight on all that luggage. It makes us look like settlers on our way to a homestead."

"But I'd hoped to look a little civilized," Mother said wistfully. "Sister Lucy and her family are coming from Virginia in their Packard, chauffeur and all. Must we arrive with a gun?"

"It's only a decoration," Father assured her. "You didn't bring any BB's, did you, Amory?"

"Just a few packages. I took out all but one extra shirt, so there was plenty of room. And anyway," Amory completed his argument, "I'd look silly with a gun and no ammunition, wouldn't I?"

No one answered. Mother tightened her lips. Father watched the ruts. And Lucy and Gwen began to plan the postcards they'd mail to people.

They drove through one tiny village after another— Union, Conway, Inkster, Orr—all very much like Wales. One town, Larimore, did have trees, like Langdon, and to Lucy trees kept a town from looking rough.

After Larimore, the morning grew longer and longer. Father didn't want to stop to eat, so Mother handed out bananas from a brown paper bag, and then a piece of Hershey chocolate to each of them. After that everyone but Father was thirsty.

"How about a drink of water from your new desert bag?" Amory asked. The canvas waterbag was hanging on the back of the Regal, but Father only shook his head, so no one else asked.

Amory kept on calling out the directions, and Mother kept on repeating them as she wrote in her log. "Turn at white schoolhouse," he read, and Mother repeated, "Turn at white schoolhouse."

Then Mother looked up and said, "But Amory, this schoolhouse has no paint at all."

Father stopped the Regal. "Well, of all the blamed mix-ups! I can't use just any old schoolhouse," Father said crossly. "If it's not white, we're off the road—could have been off for miles, too." He sounded very weary.

"Mr. Johnston, I saw another country schoolhouse back a way," said Gwen. "I remember because I thought they were awful close together when I saw this one. The other one isn't a fresh white, but it's whiter than this."

"Another school? It might be two townships with a school for each," Father began to brighten. "Why Gwendolyn Owen, I declare you've paid your round-trip fare in one day." And Father circled around the empty school yard and drove back.

Sure enough, at the other school the tall posts for the rope swings had three lines of paint, the red line between the two white ones to mark their Red Trail. It stood at a crossroads, and rounding the corner they saw another Red Trail sign on a fencepost ahead. Off they drove, on the right road again.

After a short time Amory said pathetically, "I'm so near starved that I don't think I'll be much help from now on. Couldn't we stop for just a sip of water and maybe a bite of bread?"

Lucy agreed. Her legs felt like sticks, and the visor of her touring bonnet rubbed on her forehead. "Let's stop at that coulee ahead," she suggested. "It's got some willows and we could picnic."

"It's only a dip in the prairie, but we do need a change," Father said, as he stopped the Regal at the side of the road.

Once out and sitting by the three small willows, they slowly ate their mashed lunch, no one in a hurry to return to the auto. But soon they had to jam themselves back in. They'd gone only 70 miles of their 500-mile journey. Luckily the next miles had every trail sign and every landmark exactly where it should be.

"Even after you leave Cavalier County, everything does look a lot the same, doesn't it?" commented Lucy. "I sort of thought—"

But everyone was too drowsy to ask her what she had thought. On they drove in the hot July afternoon with a hot dusty wind blowing across the fields.

Then around four o'clock the hot day turned suddenly cooler, and behind them big storm clouds rolled across the prairie sky. Everything became dark. When the clouds began to gain on them, Father stopped the auto, jumped out and called, "Everybody help put up the top!"

Tugging and hauling, the five of them pulled up the top, swung it across the auto and fastened the straps to the windshield. By that time the wind blew in strong gusts. There was a jagged fork of lightning, and then a far-off roll of thunder that reverberated over miles and miles of prairie.

"We'll put on the side curtains—just in case," said

Father. "But I won't bother with the tire chains. The storm may not hit us at all. If it does—could you three in the back take one more suitcase inside?" he asked. "Those on the trunk rack have canvas over them, but the one on the running board hasn't a hope of staying dry."

So into the backseat and onto their laps came a heavy suitcase. "What you got in this suitcase?" Lucy asked. "It's heavy as the junk that George collected."

"It really does weigh a ton, Harry," said Mother, as she took more of the weight onto her lap. "Did you add anything to it after I packed it?"

"Here comes the rain," Father said. Then he added, "About that suitcase—yes, I put in a couple of books last night."

"You're taking books? What kind of books?" Mother asked.

"One's about the species and habits of water birds. Your folks never have what I want to know," Father explained.

"Not that book as big as a dictionary?" Mother sounded startled. "Harry Johnston, you're as bad as Amory—BB guns and wildfowl books! You'd think we were on a safari."

But Mother said no more. Father was pushing the Regal over twenty, and Mother knew when to keep still. Soon with a swoosh of rain and wind, the storm hit them. For a short distance the auto kept up its speed. Then the dirt road rapidly became a gumbo track of slippery mud. The Regal barely plowed along at five miles an hour.

"At this rate," Amory said in disgust, "we won't even get there this summer. Can't you step on it?"

Perhaps Father did step on it, for the Regal slithered

around in a half-circle and then slowly slid into the ditch. Father ground the gears and shoved at the clutch and said, "Rats! Rats! Rats!" Each *Rats* was more like a swearword than the one before. Nothing worked. Finally Father turned off the engine and slumped over the wheel.

For a few moments they all sat still, with nothing to look at but the rain falling on the yellowed windows of the side curtains, and nothing to listen to but the beating of the rain on the canvas top.

"If we all took off our shoes and pushed?" suggested Lucy. "Or how about that little shack on that farm way up ahead? Might there be horses in that barn, Father?"

It was Amory and not Father who answered. "It's not pouring quite so hard now. How about my running barefoot up to that shack? I'll bet I could persuade that farmer to pull us out with his team." And Amory began taking off his shoes.

Mother said, "No shoes in the lunch basket, Amory."

And as Amory jumped out, Father said, "Tell the farmer I'll pay him a dollar if he'll bring his team soon and get us out."

"A dollar? For a man and a team? It's not hard for them. Look what I'm having to do. Got a dollar for me too?" Amory bargained. But he didn't wait for a reply. Up the sticky bank of the ditch he plodded, and then they could see him, half running and half slipping, along the muddy road to the farmyard.

"Amory really is a big brother," Gwen said admiringly. "He's an awful lot more of a do-er than Edward, isn't he?"

"Yes," Lucy agreed, "but some of Amory's doing I could do without."

By then Father had revived, and Mother had begun

to see the happier side of life. "Amory loves to go barefoot and he loves to meet strangers, so he's in his element now," she said.

"Pity his element today is water," Father grumbled. "One more deluge like this, and I'll use that log of yours to lead us home before we all drown."

"Your book on water birds was the right one," teased Mother. "What's the other book you sneaked in?"

"It's that new geology book. If we come home by way of the Red River valley, I want to follow ancient Lake Agassiz—It was over 700 miles long, and two million years ago—"

"Here comes Amory with a farmer and his team," Lucy interrupted, bringing Father back to a ditch in North Dakota in 1916.

The farmer looked almost happy to see them stuck in the mud. Before he fastened the ropes to the Regal, he stood beside it, and after a long spit of tobacco juice toward the road, he leaned in and sneered, "Youse people in autos! Always got to get a horse, ain't you?"

Then he went to the front and began fastening his team to the angle of the crank. "No!" yelled Father. "Can't you see you'll pull out the crank that way? We'll be done for!" So Father took charge of the Regal, and the farmer took charge of the team, and eventually the auto was up on the sticky road, and the man went off with his dollar in his overall pocket.

The road was so deep in mud that Father could drive only eight miles an hour, and it took so long to go from one landmark to another that Amory kept losing his place in the book. Once they went five miles in the wrong direction and had to retrace their way on a road of deep ruts and puddles, with water-filled ditches on either side.

When it was after suppertime, Amory begged, "Can't we stop to eat? I'm so hungry that I believe my stomach has shrunk. Do you think I might get stomach ulcers?"

"Not likely," said Father, "but we can't go on forever, and we can eat in the auto. Too wet everywhere else." So they sat in their cramped seats, with their elbows so close together that no one could be sure whose sandwich was going to whose mouth.

On the road again, they passed large farmhouses and big red barns but not a single town or village. "Next town should be Roseville," Amory told them.

"Sounds good, doesn't it?" Lucy said.

"It may sound good," Amory went on, "but the book says it's only one elevator on a railroad switch—no good to us."

"What's next after one-elevator Roseville?" asked Father.

"A town with three elevators—Claridge," Amory answered.

"Oh, Claridge sounds even better than Roseville," Gwen declared. "I've read in books that in London the very best hotel—you know for dukes and duchesses and earls—is the Claridge."

Lucy feared Gwen might be overestimating a three-elevator town in North Dakota, but before she could say anything, Amory spoke. "Listen to this. I just figured how many miles it is from Wales to Claridge, and you guess how many miles that will make for one day." Then he didn't wait for their guesses, but gave the astonishing figure. "A hundred and fifty miles in one day! Must be some sort of record—I mean a record for a Regal on roads like this?"

Gwen and Lucy looked at each other in amazement. Father said, "I'm not sure about the Regal record, but if I survive at all, it'll be more than a record—it'll be a miracle!"

"Once we get to Claridge, we'll go right to bed and have a long sleep," Mother said brightly.

So on they drove, mile after mile of straight section-line roads over the flat land. Twilight changed to dark. Father stopped and lit the brass-rimmed lamps, and a pale moon came up. But all around them spread the dark wide space of open prairie.

Then far ahead Lucy thought she saw three elevators against the moonlit sky. "Isn't that Claridge with our hotel?" she asked. They all looked to where she pointed and saw the three tall towers with a dim cluster of low buildings around them.

At eleven o'clock they pulled into Claridge, smaller than Wales, with fewer houses, only one church, and no cottonwoods. The main street had two stores and a ramshackle building with a crooked sign HOTEL.

There Father drew up and said, "We might as well all go in. We'll have to stay here, even if we sit all night in the lobby."

Amory pushed open the hotel door, and Lucy, right behind him, saw a wispy-haired woman in a kimono come into the bare lobby from a far door.

"Sure, I got a room," she answered Father. "You follow me." Each of them lugged a bag up a long dusty flight of stairs and then along an upstairs hall, as the woman shuffled ahead of them in old gray bedroom slippers. Everywhere the brown wallpaper was peeling and the straw matting on the floor was dirty and frayed. After they had passed four or five closed doors, the hotel owner opened a door to a big, dingy room with two beds.

"It's all I got ready tonight," she said. "The boy can

sleep with his pa and the girls with their ma." Then she held out her hand, saying, "Most of my rooms is a dollar, but this one's got so many extras—two beds and those four chairs and all—so it's two dollars. And I like the pay before folks go to bed."

Father looked at Mother. Mother stood a moment looking around the room, and Lucy looked, too. The paper was loose on the walls and so dirty that you couldn't be sure whether it had a pattern or not. The bedspreads were a stained pale blue, and the rag rugs were torn and rumpled.

Then Mother shrugged her shoulders and said, "This will do very well for one night, Harry." So Father paid and then went downstairs to find a livery stable for the Regal for the night.

"Now let's all wash up," said Mother, going over to the tall china pitcher in the china basin. "Hmmmmm! There is a little water here, but let's wash only our hands tonight. This basin has years of tide marks around it."

As soon as Father returned, they all fell into bed, and he blew out the kerosene lamp. Lucy and Gwen were asleep in no time, Lucy in the middle with Gwen on one side and Mother on the other.

Sometime later Lucy woke in the light of the lamp. Mother and Father were standing beside her bed. "Ours is alive with them!" exclaimed Father. "Bedbugs!"

"This bed is, too!" Mother was almost crying. "Look, there goes one under my pillow. We can't stay in these beds, Harry, and we can't drive on in the middle of the night, and, oh, sometimes I wish I'd never asked you to take this trip."

"There, there, Caroline," Father comforted her. "You're just exhausted." He put his arm around her. "We'll get the children up and keep the lamp lit and sit on the floor and tell stories until we can start out again."

"Tell stories!" Mother began to wipe her eyes, so Lucy knew she had been crying. "This is a story all right. Imagine arriving at my father's house with bed-bugs."

"I know what to do when you've got bedbugs," said Lucy, jumping out of bed. "You just sit up in those straight wooden chairs." And then before she thought, she used Luke's words. "Bedbugs aren't chair bugs, you know."

"How in the world, Lucy, did you become a bedbug expert?" asked Father in an amazed voice, so loud that it wakened both Gwen and Amory. So Lucy didn't have to answer him.

"What's going on?" asked Amory, sitting straight up in bed. "Gee, do I itch," he said as he scratched his chest.

"This hotel has bedbugs," Father explained very calmly. "Get out of bed, let me look you over, and then we're going to sit on these straight chairs for the rest of the night. That's the advice of your experienced sister Lucy."

Amory paid no attention to Lucy's advice. "Just wait till I tell the boys back home about being attacked by bedbugs—swarms of them. And I'll bet Aunt Lucy's children have never even seen a bedbug," Amory said.

"I should hope not," said Mother, as she began to examine Gwen and Lucy. "We'll dress now and repack so we can leave as soon as dawn comes."

"And so the bugs won't get into the bags," Amory said, imagining new horrors.

"Amory, skip the bug talk," said Mother pleadingly. "Right now I can't take it. Come on, girls, with only one chair for you two, you'll have to lean against each

other and try to sleep."

"You don't catch me going back to sleep," said Amory. "I'm going to stay awake to count bugs."

"If you can't shut your eyes, you can at least shut your mouth, Amory," Father ordered. And Amory shut up.

The rest of the night they dozed in their hard wooden chairs, but no one really slept. And as Lucy sat there half awake, she felt great sympathy for Luke Morgan.

When the first gray light of dawn appeared, they picked up their suitcases and followed Father down the barren hall and the long flight of dirty stairs and out the front door to the empty street.

Father brought the Regal from the livery stable and they silently piled in. As they drove off, Lucy said to herself, "That's one town that must be rougher than Wales. I wonder if it's wickeder."

Amory Disappears

For the first few miles after Claridge, Mother and Father were so silent that no one else spoke either. Then Amory said, "I've read two pages ahead—not a single town where we can get breakfast." Then he read aloud, "Four miles, turn where road turns. Two and a half miles, watch for church."

"Maybe it isn't in the book, but there's one elevator over there on the right," Lucy said.

"According to the book, it isn't there," Amory said.

"We might be off the trail," suggested Lucy.

"Again?" Father said in a very discouraged voice. Then he went on more cheerfully, "That certainly is an elevator. Might be a village with some place to get something hot to eat." And he turned the Regal toward the one elevator.

Soon they were in a village of a few small houses, one store, and a tiny restaurant near the railroad. As they entered the place, they immediately faced a long hanging spiral of sticky flypaper, dotted with dead flies. Mother started to back out the door, but Father took her by the arm and led her to a small table, saying, "I know dead flies aren't appetizing before breakfast, but they do show that the owner is trying to run a clean place."

When a tidy pink-cheeked woman in a starched apron came in from the kitchen, Mother relaxed. They all had ham and eggs with fat buttered rolls, and Mother and Father each had two big mugs of coffee.

Back in the auto, Amory said, "You and your dukes and duchesses can have the Claridge, Gwen. I'm all for an eating joint like that one."

"But that Claridge woman did tell the truth," Lucy reminded him. "Remember she told us that room had all the extras?"

"Extras, all right!" joked Father, now back in a good mood. "So many extras that we couldn't count them."

"Father, what about the Wales hotel?" Lucy asked. "I've been wondering—what's it like? At night, I mean."

"Well, Mrs. Moors works hard, she tells me, trying to keep a couple of rooms spotless for people she knows are spotless, but—"

Amory interrupted Father. "But if you're not spotless, pow! you're eaten alive!"

"Would all of you mind getting off that subject?" asked Mother. "I can't stand one more—"

Then Amory interrupted Mother, "My gun! Where's my gun? Who's sitting on it now? Or did we leave it for bugs?"

"Your gun's fastened on the trunk rack, Amory, and

if you can't stop talking about those you-know-whats, your mother is likely to have you fastened back there, too."

Amory started to argue, but a look at Father's jaw told him to read the guidebook instead. "That hick town was off the trail all right," he said. "Now we go one mile east and one and a half miles south past a farm with a silo. Then east again past a red schoolhouse, and we'll be where we should be, or I think so," he ended, rather uncertainly.

He needn't have worried. The silo and later the red schoolhouse were where they should be, and the stripes were on a telephone pole and on a fencepost as well.

"Straight on to Fargo!" Amory called out.

"I can hardly wait," Lucy said. "You'd say it's a city, wouldn't you, Father?"

"Yes, shops and pavement and streetlights," answered Father, "but we may go on farther before we stop for the night."

"Harry, unless it holds you up too long, tonight I'd like to stay at a place where the water runs in a basin instead of in a ditch," Mother said wistfully.

"Fine. Fargo it shall be. That is," added Father, "if the Regal continues to speed along and it doesn't rain again and we don't get off the trail and we don't get a flat."

"Don't even breathe the word *flat*," begged Mother.

"Must be wonderful to live in a city like Fargo," said Lucy. "Doesn't it have buildings five stories high?"

"Yes, but don't forget that Wales has six elevators, all a lot higher than that," said Father, who always wanted Wales to get its fair share of praise.

"But grain elevators are for grain, and not people," Lucy insisted.

Later, in the afternoon, they drove along the paved streets of Fargo and stopped in front of a big brick hotel. Inside, the lobby had marble columns, overstuffed chairs with overstuffed men smoking cigars, and everywhere bellhops hurrying here and there in their bright orange jackets with gold braid.

Going up in the elevator to their fourth-floor room, Amory asked so many questions of the wizened old man who ran it that the man laughed and asked, "Plan to run an elevator when you're big, sonny?"

"Nope, but I want a lot of rides in it while I'm here," Amory answered.

Again, their room was a big one with two double beds, but everything else was different from the Claridge room. The fresh yellow wallpaper, the white curtains, the two soft armchairs—everything met with Mother's approval. "This is more like it," she said. And Lucy agreed.

Quickly they all washed and changed, but as Mother took a clean gingham dress for Lucy from her suitcase, out rolled Clarissa, wrapped in her layers of wardrobe. Mother looked as though she'd seen a ghost. "Lucy!" she scolded. "You brought Clarissa? Why you don't even play with dolls anymore!" Then Mother's eyes narrowed. "Tell me, what did you leave at home to make room for this display?"

"Well, Mother, Aunt Lucy gave me Clarissa and I wanted to show her how well I can featherstitch and sew on ruffles, and the only things I could leave out were my button shoes and my extra black stockings, and anyway, how could I take Clarissa's clothes without her to model them, and there's the blue-and-white plaid dress and that—"

"For goodness' sake, Lucy. Stop talking," Mother

cut in. "You've got Clarissa here with all her wardrobe, but you've only got that one pair of shoes you have on, so mind—don't get them wet." Then she turned to Father and asked, "You didn't leave anything out to get in those two heavy books, did you?"

"No," said Father, pawing around in the big suitcase, "but I can't find my other pair of trousers."

"Oh, dear," said Mother, "I was sure I put them under that big brown folder. Aren't they there?"

"Here they are," said Father, pulling them out, and with them he pulled out the brown folder. All over the floor spilled pages of printed music, inked pages of Mother's own music, and blank lined pages for her to write more music.

"What in tarnation, Caroline," Father thundered. And then he began to chuckle. "Here you've been scolding us for bringing our heavy things from home, and all the time you had this load of music. Talk about a dishonest character, you do take the cake!" And he began laughing so hard he couldn't go on.

"But Harry," Mother tried to explain, "one of the things I'm going for is to make music with my sisters."

"It's all right! It's all right! Only don't you scold us anymore, will you?" Father gave her a kiss, and she began to laugh along with him. "Now let's all go to the nearest dime store before it closes," he said, and no one argued against that.

Around the corner was a Woolworth's, and Father was so delighted with all he could buy for a dime that he gave each of them a dime to buy postcards and then thirty cents apiece for anything they wanted. Gwen bought giant pencils to take home to her family, all identical so that Edward couldn't complain. Amory got a book called *King Solomon's Mines* that Father said

was a "humdinger of a mystery story." Lucy, not seeing anything she really wanted for herself, bought a
celluloid doll for Hilda, with two little dresses and tiny
white socks and shoes.

Back at their room, they had time to write their
cards before supper. Lucy planned to send one to each
of the twins as well as to Hilda, but she suddenly thought
of Toby Shaw, and feeling she must leave no stone unturned, she used one to say, "Dear Mr. Toby Shaw,
Luke is waiting for you so he can join the army. Hurry
up! Yours truly," but then she didn't want to sign her
name, so she left it at that. Then the address—she was
still puzzling over that, when Father said, "Off we go
for supper."

So she hastily scrawled, "Mr. Toby Shaw, Care of
Bradna's Dogs, Barnum-Bailey Circus, Minneapolis, Minnesota." Sending a card to a man in care of dogs did
seem odd, but at least for next Saturday she knew the
circus was in Minneapolis, so mail might be delivered.

For supper they went to a busy cafeteria, the first one
Lucy had ever been to. She grew more and more ner-
vous as they moved up to the counter, so that when she
arrived at the food, she took the first thing she saw—a
big plate of gummy macaroni.

Amory had no problems. He raided the counter for
three main dishes—corned beef hash, frankfurters and
mashed potatoes, and roast pork with applesauce. Mother
shook her head at him, but he only grinned at her and
loaded the edges of his tray with three desserts—a chunk
of frosted chocolate cake, the biggest piece of apple pie
in sight, and a double scoop of maple nut ice cream.

The two girls chose the ice cream, and as Gwen licked
her last spoonful, she said to Lucy, "This drive has been
so good," she stopped. "Well, just so good! And when

you pick me up next week, you must tell me every single thing that happens on the rest of the trip."

"Even if it's another Claridge?" Lucy asked, and they giggled, until Mother broke in with a firm, "Forget Claridge!"

Later, when they set out to cross the Red River and take Gwen to Moorhead, Amory stayed at the hotel to read his new book. The family in Moorhead had more children than Lucy had expected. They swarmed all over the front yard, paying no attention to anyone. Lucy decided Gwen's week of babysitting would be mostly baby running. Then all three of them kissed Gwen good-bye, and she and Lucy waved to each other until the auto was around the corner.

Back at the hotel, they were so tired they went directly to the elevator to go up to bed. "Elevator's broken down," a bellhop told them. So they walked up the three flights of stairs and were more ready for bed than ever.

Opening their bedroom door, Mother called, "Amory, we're back, and we're all going to bed." There was no answer. Both the beds and the two big armchairs were empty.

"Probably he's down the hall in the bathroom," Father said. But after half an hour, Father agreed with Mother that Amory seldom stayed that long in one place, especially a bathroom.

By now they were all three in bed, but Father got up and dressed. "I'll find him, Caroline, though I do wish he weren't such a slippery character to keep track of."

"Don't call him slippery," corrected Mother. "That sounds dishonest." But Father was out in the hall, and the door was shut.

After nearly an hour, Father returned, without

Amory. "He's simply disappeared," said Father. "I've been up and down every corridor and then outside along every nearby block. And no one has seen him." Father sank into one of the big chairs. "I'll rest and then go out again. Trouble is that I'm so blamed tired."

Mother got up then and began dressing. "We can't let Amory ramble on strange city streets," she said. "He's probably frightened and confused and perhaps really lost. Poor child, his birthday's tomorrow."

"What's his birthday got to do with it?" Father asked sharply. "And wherever he is, he's not frightened and confused. He's got a sense of direction that would do credit to a homing pigeon!"

"I'm going out to look anyway," Mother said, and out she went.

Lucy was now the only one in bed, and she shivered a little thinking of Amory out alone, lost on city streets.

After a while Father stood up. "Lucy, you'll have to stay here alone while I go out to find both your mother and Amory. Never saw such a footloose bunch."

"Wait for me, Father!" Lucy hopped out of bed and began to dress. "I want to go along too."

"Sure, I'll wait," Father said. "Might as well lose the whole family at once—not worth much anyway."

Out in the hall, with her clothes tossed on any old way, Lucy began thinking of places Amory might be. "Did you look in the hotel dining room? Or the kitchen, Father? Does a hotel have any booths for shooting or taking chances? Or a place for games? You know how much Amory likes games."

By now the lighted arrows were flashing over the elevator, so they waited for it. It stopped at their floor, the door opened, and Amory bounded out.

"Where you two going?" he asked before they could

say a word. "Let me come, too. I got some more money to spend—a whole lot. Any store open now, so I could buy things?"

"Amory Johnston, where have you been?" Father barked in his loudest voice.

"I just went for a ride on the elevator, and when it got to the basement, something broke. And down there some men were shaking dice, and—"

Amory was interrupted by Mother, who came hurrying along the hall. "Where on earth have you been, Amory?" Mother was furious. "I've looked everywhere for you, and I came back to ask your father to phone the police and— Where have you been?" she repeated.

"Right here in the hotel. I didn't go out wandering on the streets the way you've been doing. I just watched those men playing, and I asked if I could too and they said 'Why not?' So I did and look here," and Amory pulled from his pocket two silver dollars and a silver fifty-cent piece.

"That's gambling, Amory," Father said in a shocked voice. "We'll go right down and return this money at once," and Father took him by the arm and started for the stairs.

"Oh, they've all gone to work in the kitchen now, and they'd be in trouble if anybody knew they—well, anyway they had more money than this—stacks of it, and besides, I couldn't find them now." The complications stopped even Father, so Amory won his argument and kept his silver money.

"Well, come to bed—all of you," Father said. "We're all worn out."

"But I'm not tired," Amory insisted. "And I haven't finished my book yet."

"Tonight you go to bed and be certain to stay there,"

Father commanded.

"But I want to go out and spend some of this money. Tomorrow's my birthday. Remember? I could buy myself an extra present or two," Amory begged. "Might be a store open."

"Tomorrow, Amory, you'll be lucky if you don't get a birthday spanking of a lot more than twelve spanks and one to grow on," said Mother in a very unfunny tone, as they all went down the hall to their room and to bed.

Lucy Loses Her Shoe

At five o'clock in the morning, Lucy called to Amory, "Happy Birthday!" He didn't waken, so she tried again. "Happy Birthday! and we brought along presents for you." That woke him up in no time at all. Mother gave him a pocket compass that Lucy had seen before they left home, but Father's present was a real surprise—a four-bladed jackknife with a fish scaler, a fingernail file, and a corkscrew.

About the compass, Father said, "Your mother doesn't want to lose you again, does she?" And about the knife, Mother said, "Mind you don't cut the wrong things, and I hope you grow up to use the fingernail file more than the corkscrew."

Then Lucy held out the new wallet, warning him, "It's empty, Amory. You'll have to fill it yourself."

"Cash is no problem," Amory told her. "I've got all that money I earned last night—two dollars and fifty cents—and I brought that dollar bill I earned at the shooting booth."

"You didn't earn a cent of that money," Lucy said bitterly. "You just win money, and I work for what I get."

"Work? You work? A girl doesn't really work," Amory said.

Before Lucy could answer, Father stopped the argument. "No squabbling, especially on a birthday. And Amory, you can carry the bill in your wallet, but the silver I'm putting in the suitcase. That way you just might have a little of your hard-earned cash left when you get to Minnetonka."

Soon they were on the road again. Whether it was because it was a birthday or because it was time for better luck, the day was sunny and the driving was so easy that Father even bellowed the old Sunday school song, "Brighten the Corner Where You Are." Lucy thought it pretty childish of him, but at least everyone was in a good mood.

By noon they had covered eighty miles, after two stops at real garages, once to have the mud pan wired on again and once to fill the Regal's tank with gasoline. Then out on the open road, Father said, "Time I greased the auto. I shouldn't drive it another mile." Father never trusted anyone else to grease the Regal. He carried his own tin of grease and a little squirt gun to shoot it into the places that Amory identified by a sheet of instructions and a diagram.

"Can't we drive to that farm up ahead?" asked Mother. "There's a windmill, so they must have a well. We could get a drink of water to go with our crackers and cheese and the raspberries we bought." When Father didn't agree at once, she went on. "I hate to say it, Harry, but the water from that canvas desert bag you bought tastes like the bottom of the barrel."

Then Lucy objected to the farmhouse. "Look, Mother, part of that house is just a tarpaper shack, and we've gone by beautiful white houses with porches and fresh paint."

Lucy's objections decided Father. "You look too much at the paint, Lucy. That farmhouse ahead will be fine. And look—there's as good an auto as ours, right at the door." So they drove into the weedy yard, and the chickens squawked off in all directions and an old dog barked.

Just then a man in a dark gray suit came out the door, carrying a doctor's black leather satchel. He stopped beside his Ford as the Regal drew up to the house. "You people better not go in," he said. "Amelia's got infantile."

Then he looked more closely at them. "Oh, you people are strangers, aren't you? Well, Amelia's the only kid they've got—about eight years old. She hasn't got it bad, but if I were you, I wouldn't stay around," he said.

"Certainly, we'll leave right away. But is there anything we can do?" asked Mother, looking toward the tall woman now leaning against the doorpost. Then at the window Lucy saw the face of a pale little girl.

The doctor saw her too, and he yelled to the woman, "Keep her in bed, like I told you."

"She's got nothing to do in bed," the woman yelled.

"I wonder if we have something we could leave for her," Mother said almost to herself. Then she asked the doctor, "Would she like a doll, do you think?" The doctor nodded.

Lucy went rigid. Mother was a very giving person, but would she really give away Clarissa, just like that? To live the rest of her doll life in a tarpaper shack, and with all those specially designed new clothes?

"Reach into the picnic basket, Amory, and hand me the doll Lucy bought for Hilda. I put it there last night," Mother said. So Amory handed the doll to Mother, who made sure it had its complete outfit. Then she handed it to the doctor to hand to the woman to hand to the little girl inside the house.

Only after they were back on the main road, did Mother speak to Lucy. "We'll get something else for Hilda. I'm sorry I didn't even ask you—but you know—infantile's so terribly catching." Mother sounded frightened.

"It was like a story I read once about the plague," Lucy said, "and how people wouldn't go near anyone else."

"Goodness, Lucy, don't think that way," Mother told her. "They had a doctor. We couldn't help, and you children run a great risk if you get too close."

Then Amory had to bring in his reading. "In my volume on ancient history there was a whole page about a plague in Athens, and do you know what people looked like when they caught it?"

"Skip it, Amory," Father said. "Sometimes what happens right around us is enough without dredging into history." So no one said anything more about either infantile or the plague.

A mile farther on they found a level place where Father and Amory greased the auto, and they all munched on crackers and cheese and no one complained of having only dark-red raspberries to quench their thirst.

As they packed up to start again, the sun went under a cloud and the day changed to a threatening one. It wasn't raining, but far ahead a rain cloud was building up. Father began to drive the Regal at its top speed. Then with a thump and a bump the auto began to wobble on the narrow dirt road. A flat tire. And a storm ahead.

Everybody helped take everything out from the metal rack on the running board to uncover the black tin toolbox. Father got down on his knees, pushed the jack under the rear wheel, slowly lifted the Regal, jerked the tire off the rim, and yanked out the inner tube. He found the leak at once, opened his repair kit, smeared the tube with sticky cement and pressed a rubber patch over the leak.

But it was useless. As fast as he mended one spot and had Amory use the hand pump to fill the tube with air, another place hissed out a new leak.

Father shook his head, pressed on another patch and tried again and again. By the fifth try, Mother spoke very mildly. "Harry, where's the brand new tube you bought for the trip?"

"That's for an emergency," Father replied severely.

Mother exploded. "We've spent over an hour here, there's a storm coming up, and that tube you're mending hasn't a place left for you to stick one more patch. If this isn't an emergency, what in heaven's name is?" And she waited for him to answer.

"Well, I was thinking of an emergency like our being out late at night again and having a flat," Father said.

"We'll not be out on the road again after dark if I have anything to say about it," Mother said. "Put in that new tube—now!"

So Father put the new tube in the casing, soon everything was repacked and they were on their way again. The split tube was tied on the trunk rack—"in case of a worse emergency," Father insisted.

Before long the rainstorm met them head on. They already had the top up, but by the time the side curtains were buttoned on, it was too late for Father to put on the chains without getting soaked. The road quickly became a slosh of mud and ruts of running water, and in the first low swampy spot, the Regal stuck in the deepest, stickiest mudhole.

Father soon gave up trying to drive out of it, and he clicked off the engine in disgust. "This snake belly of an underslung Regal," he muttered so it sounded like swearing. "One of Henry Ford's tin Lizzies could navigate this, but we're stuck for good."

"This road's so narrow that anyone coming along will have to help us or they can't pass," Mother said encouragingly.

"There hasn't been another auto or even a horse for miles," Father answered. "Back a way I saw some ramshackle buildings, so we'll sit until the rain lets up, then off you go, Amory, to the rescue again."

"Not Amory. I'd almost rather go myself," Mother said. "Amory might disappear again."

"Nonsense! Amory won't get lost in a desolate place like this, will you?" Father asked.

"How much do we pay for a team this time?" was Amory's reply.

"Mother," Lucy exclaimed, "there's a leak in the top—and it's right over my bonnet!"

"Take it off before it's soaked, dear," Mother soothed her. "Amory, you pass her a flat enamel cup from the picnic basket, and she can hold it over her head."

So for a time they sat, hearing the rain drumming on

the top and an occasional *ping* of a drop falling into Lucy's cup. When it was raining less, Amory took off his shoes and stockings, pulled his knickerbockers high on his legs, and began his slippery run back to the farm buildings.

Before many minutes had passed, he was running toward them again, alone. "Nobody there," he shouted as he came nearer. "The windows are all broken, and there's nothing inside. Even the barn's empty—empty—empty!" Amory half sang it three times for emphasis.

"What'll we do?" moaned Lucy, looking out on the deep mud of the road and the miles and miles of soaked fields all around them.

"This time we push ourselves out," replied Father grimly. "I'll crank the engine. Caroline, you sit behind the wheel and steer. I'll roll up my trousers, and Lucy, take off your shoes and stockings. The three of us must push and shove and push again."

The mudhole was so deep that they kept sinking in to their ankles, and when the wheels spun, the slick mud sprayed all over their legs. But the pushing finally worked, and the Regal stood on a drier piece of the road.

Lucy and Amory were so muddy when they climbed back in, both barefoot, that Mother said, "Don't put such feet into stockings or shoes. And Lucy," she added, "please stay in that corner of the seat by yourself. You're a heroine for helping, but you look more like a mud pie."

For that night they stayed in Benson, Minnesota. Father first inspected the hotel and pronounced it very clean, so clean that he wondered if such a muddy family would be welcome. But the smiling fat man with a gold watch chain across his vest welcomed them all in. He was the ideal hotel owner.

"Come right upstairs. I've got kettles of hot water ready for washing up. You're the only people here to-night, so when you're ready for supper, come on down to the kitchen and eat with me and my daughter," he invited.

When everyone was scraped and washed and dried, Lucy discovered her shoes were missing. "I must have left my shoes in the auto," she said.

"Put on your other pair for now," Mother answered. Then she looked unhappy. "Oh, I forgot. Clarissa replaced your other pair, didn't she? Harry, I hate to ask you," Mother went on, "but while the Regal is still in front of the hotel, would you go down and get Lucy's shoes?"

So Father went down to the auto and was soon back in the room. "Here's one shoe," he said, holding it out, "but the other must have fallen out at the mudhole. Hop along in one shoe, Lucy. We'll explain your problem. We don't want you to get splinters from these wooden floors." So Lucy hopped.

After the rain, it had turned colder, and they were glad to eat at one end of the long wooden table in the middle of the warm kitchen. When the young woman in the pink plaid dress heard it was Amory's birthday, she brought out vanilla ice cream and part of a huge angel cake.

As she put a gigantic piece on Amory's plate, she winked at Lucy. "I'll bet he's no angel, is he?"

Mother was perhaps afraid of what Lucy might answer, for she immediately said, "Well, everybody loves him, but I've never heard anyone call him an angel."

"If they did, I'd hit them in the snoot," Amory said, grinning. "All those white wings and long sissy skirts!"

"Just as I thought," said the hotelkeeper's daughter.

Upstairs again, even Amory was tired enough to go to bed, only asking first to count his silver money once more and keep it on his bedside table for the night.

Lucy undressed swiftly, but as she laid out the clothes she'd put on the next day to meet the city cousins, she faced that one lonesome shoe. "Mother, whatever can I do? Imagine how I'll look with only one shoe. Can't we stop somewhere tomorrow and buy me a new pair of shoes?" she begged.

Father gave the answer. "Definitely not. Tomorrow we're on the homestretch, and we're going to stay on it until we get there, even if we all arrive barefoot."

"And with bedbugs!" yelled Amory.

"Hush!" Mother was almost as loud as Amory. "If you keep on talking about that, I'm never going to be able to face my family," Mother said. Then to Lucy she added, "Except for your Aunt Frances's son Gale, you'll be the youngest cousin there, you know, so you could be barefoot, if you like."

"Better yet, Lucy," Father chuckled, "wear your one shoe. That'll show them that even in Wales we do buy shoes."

"Don't laugh," Lucy said. "It's not funny for me." And she thought of those two young lady cousins, Minerva and Frances, and pictured them laughing at her.

"It won't kill you to arrive in one shoe, Lucy, though I hadn't planned for us to look quite so much like refugees." Mother half sighed.

Up at dawn and repacking and having a hotel breakfast had become usual for Lucy. "This must be the way gypsies live," she told herself. And that made her think of the gypsy fortune-teller at the fair. "Going on a journey to find happiness—" Fine idea of happiness,

Lucy thought, to soak your bonnet because of a hole in the top, and lose your shoe in the mud, and perhaps pick up bedbugs—but no, she'd better forget those.

The fourth day's drive was speeding almost all the way. They could arrive at Grandfather Gale's in time for evening dinner if they hurried, so again their lunch was only crackers, cheese, and fruit that Father bought at a little crossroads store.

The only crisis of the day came when Amory suddenly shouted, "My silver money! Did you put it back in the suitcase?" And when both Mother and Father remembered seeing it last on the bedside table, Amory was in a panic. "You left my silver? How could you do that to me?"

"Seems to me you did it to yourself," Father said. "You got it out, and you left it, not me. That hotelman's daughter will think we're very generous people to leave such a good tip."

"Generous people!" Amory raged. "Everybody gives away my cash." He turned to face Lucy. "And I won't forget you gave away my ten-dollar prize. That was even worse! And now you sit there with your big mouth grinning like a jack-o'-lantern, and—and—nobody helps me save my money," he howled.

"It's gone, so keep still," Father said.

"And you can just remember," Mother preached, "cash you get that way is 'Easy come, easy go.'"

That was the end of the talk, but Lucy sat wishing that Amory hadn't mentioned her wide mouth. Mother always said such a wide mouth made a nice wide smile, but who wants to look like Alice in Wonderland's Cheshire cat? And probably Minerva and Frances had beautiful small mouths.

By late afternoon they saw a low line of city smudge

along the horizon. "That's Minneapolis," Father said. "Good thing Lake Minnetonka is on this side of it—traffic I can't take, and you can have the city, too."

A little while longer, and Mother called out, "Here's the curve in the road, and here's the corner—and there it is!" The big summer home came into sight, and Lucy, hearing the quiver in Mother's voice, realized how much this trip meant to Mother. It was her first summer visit with her father and her two sisters and their families for many years.

Five More Cousins

W e'll park back here at the edge of the garden," Father said. Amory reached over, and before Father could stop him, he gave three massive squeezes to the rubber bulb of their horn. So with a great honking they drew up beside the long sleek automobile of Aunt Lucy's family from Virginia. It was a seven-passenger Packard twin-six, as shiny as if it had been kept in tissue paper.

Immediately their young chauffeur, Joe, appeared on the far side of the Packard, where he must have been polishing wheels. He was smartly dressed and far cleaner than the Johnstons were at the end of a long day's riding. And he stood and stared at the dirt-caked Regal, crammed with suitcases and people.

"Hello," said Father. "So the Turnbulls are already here. Have a good trip?"

"Yes, sir," answered Joe. "Five days on the road, about 1,500 miles." He smiled proudly.

"Five days and you went 1,500 miles?" Amory echoed. "Why, we've been four days and we've gone only 500! But then, ours is only a Regal." And as he said it, the poor little Regal shrank even more in Lucy's eyes.

By now people of all sizes were running from the house. For a minute, sitting in the Regal with her one shoe, Lucy saw Mother's family as though in one large photograph.

There was white-haired Grandfather Gale, hugging Mother and laughing. He had a bristly small moustache like Father's, only white, of course. And near him were Aunt Lucy, like Mother but darker, and her tall blond husband, Uncle Albert Turnbull, and their two big daughters, Minerva and Frances, who might laugh at Lucy and at Wales. The girls had long dark hair held back from their faces with enormous bows of ribbon, and their white skirts almost touched the ground.

Next to Amory stood the two Turnbull boys, Robert, not much older than Amory but very much taller, and blond Albert, only a little older than Lucy. The whole Turnbull family was dressed in spotless linen, and of course, they wore their shoes in pairs. Poor Lucy, she felt worse than a country cousin.

Mother's widowed sister, Aunt Frances Chapman, and her boy, eight-year-old Gale, were still in the house. "Gale helped Joe polish the auto so he's changing his clothes," Aunt Lucy explained.

Lucy still sat in the backseat of the Regal, hesitant about getting out on her single shoe. Yet she knew she couldn't spend the whole six days in the backseat, so she got out and stood behind Mother, like a one-legged statue. Finally Mother took notice of her. "Our Lucy lost a shoe in the mud yesterday, and she left her other pair at home," Mother said.

"Could she wear a pair of Albert's?" asked Cousin Frances, the younger of the girls. Then as she came up and looked at the shoeless foot, she laughed. "Why you've got a Cinderella foot. We'll have to find a glass slipper for you, and they're very rare, you know." Lucy wanted to hug her for the compliment, but when you're balanced on one leg you can't do much else.

Aunt Lucy immediately took charge of the shoe problem. "Robert, go ask your Aunt Frances to bring a pair of Gale's white shoes for Lucy. Now run." And Robert ran. Lucy decided at once that she was named for someone who must always know what to do and how to get it done.

Back came Robert, with Aunt Frances hurrying behind him, carrying a pair of low white shoes. Beside her ran Gale, as spick-and-span as the Flints back home. But Lucy already had a feeling that none of these people worried about keeping clean the way Mrs. Flint did. Maybe her cousins wouldn't ever be as scornful of Wales as Mrs. Flint.

While Cousin Frances fitted her into Gale's shoes, Lucy watched everyone trooping toward the tall wooden house. Amory must already feel at home with the boys, for he was loudly telling them about the trip. "Bet you didn't stop overnight at a hotel like one we went to," he boasted. "Packed in two beds, we all went to sleep and boom! Do you know what came out of the walls to attack us?" Lucy couldn't hear the rest, but she didn't need to.

Into the house they all swarmed, through the big rough-boarded living room and up the stairs. When they were partway up, Mother paused to say to Lucy, "Look down at the sitting room furniture, dear. Those shiny flowered slipcovers are chintz. Remember?"

Mother went quickly on upstairs, but Lucy stood a moment, thinking of chintz and of the stone house and the Owens and Topsy. Wales seemed very far away. Could she possibly be homesick for that rough wicked little town?

But Father was right behind her on the stairs. "Don't stand there dreaming," he said. "These bags weigh tons."

As she hurried up the rest of the stairs, she glimpsed the dining room through the doorway. The maid, Christine, was putting extra places at the big oval table and pushing the tall candlesticks a little farther apart.

At dinner, the three big boys sat at a small side table, and they had plenty to talk about. So had the big people. But Lucy sat between her girl cousins and said little more than "Yes" or "No" to their questions about the trip, about Wales, and about herself.

Finally Cousin Frances asked, "I suppose you have a pet at home?"

Father, who was sitting nearby, said, "Lucy, tell them about Topsy, your miracle dog."

So Lucy told of Topsy's brains and her waltzing and wearing a doll's bonnet, "even when she jumped through a hoop to chase a cat." And she began to giggle, as she remembered Topsy's flying exit from the barn circus.

Frances next asked if she had friends in Wales, and Lucy launched into a roll call of the Owens. By the time she had listed Gwendolyn, Gwinyth, Guinevere, and their brother, Edward Albert Christian Owen, named for the Prince of Wales, she saw everyone around the table had stopped talking and was listening. As soon as she saw all those eyes focused on her, she shut up like a clam and said no more.

Then Grandfather began to talk. "Now tomorrow, what are you all planning? I'm going into the city for the day, and Albert, I know you have to go to northern Minnesota on business for a few days—but the rest of you? What's on your calendar?"

"It's been planned for weeks," said Aunt Frances. "We three sisters are invited to Ellen's for a luncheon, and Minerva and Frances are invited too—sort of a coming-out party for them."

"And Uncle Harry said he'd take us three older boys fishing," called Robert from the boys' table.

"Oh, do be careful, Harry," Aunt Lucy said to Father. "You've never had those three boys in one rowboat before."

"Don't you worry," teased Father. "If anybody falls overboard, I'll just hook him out with a fishpole. Gives a boy confidence to fall overboard and be fished out." Lucy noticed that Aunt Lucy looked more worried than amused, and Aunt Frances looked smug that Gale was too young to go.

"Fine! Everything's settled." Grandfather said, "except for Gale and Lucy. Christine can watch over them." Lucy wondered about having a maid "watch over" her, but she wasn't given a choice.

"Now while you three sisters are here this week,"

Grandfather went on, "I want each of you to pick one piece of furniture for your own homes. Pretty soon, you know, I've got to sell this place."

For a moment no one spoke. And though there had never been a summer home in Lucy's life, she could understand their sadness about selling a house that was almost a part of the family.

Then Mother spoke to break the sadness. "I've always wanted the cherry secretary. We need those glassed-in shelves."

"Glad you chose that, Caroline," Father broke in. "Four more shelves for my books."

"No, those shelves will be for my best china, and the drawers beneath for my table linen," Mother quickly said. Then she asked Grandfather, "Did anyone ever find that recipe for happiness that your grandmother said was hidden in it?"

"Never did," answered Grandfather, and he began to laugh. "Remember when you three were little girls and I helped you search for it all one rainy afternoon? And your mother came home before we'd put anything back? Stuff was dumped all over the parlor floor—didn't exactly make her happy, or us either."

When the laughter had ceased, Gale asked, "But is that recipe still in it?"

"It should be in it. No one has ever found it, so no one has taken it out. And my grandmother wouldn't have told a lie," answered Grandfather.

Leaving the dining room soon after, Lucy edged over to Gale and whispered, "Tomorrow when we're here alone, let's hunt for the secret in the secretary." She was glad he nodded "Yes," because "the secret in the secretary" sounded marvelously mysterious.

That evening they all stayed in the sitting room.

Amory and the boys set up the Parchesi board and began an endless round of games. Since only four could play, Mother suggested to Lucy that she exhibit Clarissa's traveling wardrobe. Later, after every costume had been properly admired, Aunt Frances asked, "Who ever taught you to sew, Lucy? Your mother is so much better at the piano than she is at the sewing machine."

"Yes, and because she's left-handed, she always begins my seams sort of upside down," Lucy said.

"Poor girl! I suppose you have to stand on your head to finish them?" asked Uncle Albert.

Since it was the first thing he had said to her, Lucy at first took him seriously. "No, not quite. No, that's not—" Lucy began, then she saw by his grin that he was teasing her. After that she felt much more at home, so she laughed and went on. "Really it's Mrs. Owen who taught me. She even makes their winter coats and Mr. Owen's suits."

"Mrs. Owen! The mother of the Prince of Wales has to make coats and suits?" Uncle Albert pretended to be shocked. "I thought a queen only sat on a throne and behaved herself as a queen should."

"Oh, not all queens behave themselves, Uncle Albert," Amory interrupted. "You should read about the goings-on of Catherine the Great of Russia, or about all those wives of King Henry the Eighth of England or about—"

"Surely you don't learn that kind of thing in the Wales school, do you, Amory?" Grandfather asked, trying to stop the royal scandals before Amory got down to details.

"It's all in Ridpath's *History of the World*," Lucy said. "But you have to know where to look, Amory says."

"And if that sounds too bookish, I fear he also knows every exciting event in Wales—at first hand, too," Father added.

"But I missed the tornado last month, and only that scaredy-cat Lucy was home then. And I missed the raid on the blind pig too, but all of us missed that," Amory said.

"A blind pig? What could happen to a blind pig?" Minerva asked quite seriously. Both Lucy and Amory stared at her. Imagine that, Lucy thought, she's almost a woman and she's ready for college and she doesn't know any more about a blind pig than Guinnie Owen did. So Father defined a blind pig for Minerva and the other cousins, too. "My goodness," Minerva said.

"And does Wales have a lot of things like that going on?" asked Robert enviously.

"All the time," Amory answered. "But let's finish this game. I'm ahead." And the boys went back to Parchesi and the grown-ups sat talking of all kinds of things, with Lucy listening to every word.

Soon Mother was telling of Karlie's death, and when she said, "So Lucy ran to get the doctor," Aunt Lucy turned to her namesake.

"And you got the doctor! What an extraordinary experience for my little Lucy."

"Well, no, I didn't get the doctor. I only ran to try to get the doctor." Lucy wanted to be honest. "But I couldn't get him because he was drunk and his wife wouldn't let him out. So I had to run for Mrs. Sanderson—a special kind of nurse, a born nurse, you know." Lucy was finally talking, and though everyone was looking at her, this time she barged right on.

"And Mrs. Sanderson really saved the new baby's life, didn't she, Mother? You see when Baby Charlie was born that afternoon, he hadn't been nine months in his mother's womb, only seven. So of course he's delicate, but I've already stayed with him—all by myself, and I had to rock him in his box." Lucy stopped. She could see that she'd made an effect of the kind only Amory usually made.

The two big girls looked at her in amazement. And Aunt Lucy said, "For heaven's sake!" Then to Mother she said, "Caroline, do you realize your Lucy won't be eleven until next month, but she's had experiences our grown daughters have never had?"

And Father answered, "Yes, if you want your children to learn independence, send them out to Wales." And he said it proudly.

But when Lucy looked at Minerva and Frances and thought of Wales, she knew it wouldn't work. Yet, there was something about life in Wales that made you decide things for yourself. And she thought of Luke and her helping him escape across the border. Now, if she told about that—even Amory would listen.

Soon it was time for Lucy to go up to bed in the little cot in her folks' room. There she lay awake for a long time, listening to Mother and Aunt Lucy playing duets on the piano and Aunt Frances singing song after song, some of them songs that Mother had composed at the old black piano at home. So that night, Lucy fell asleep to music.

Early the next morning Father and the big boys ate a whopping big breakfast in the kitchen and went off in the rowboat with piles of fishing gear and enough lunch for the whole day.

Then the rest of the family had their dining room breakfast. After that there was a great pressing of long white dresses, and white shoes were made whiter and big silk hair ribbons were tied tighter and tan linen dusters were put on to protect the dresses. Aunt Frances sewed new trimming on Mother's blue voile best dress, and Aunt Lucy loaned her a big summer hat with velvet bows and bunches of violets. Mother no longer looked like Mother, but she did look very nice, Lucy thought, as she saw them all drive off in the Packard.

"Let's start hunting for the secret," Gale said at once. At the tall secretary in the sitting room, he looked up at all the old leather books. "First we look in every book," he mapped the search. He turned the brass key in the many-paned doors, and they set to work.

As he handed down volume after volume, Lucy leafed through each one, and stacked them in toppling piles around her. By the time they came to the top shelf, Lucy suggested, "Maybe we're on the wrong track. Didn't they say it was inside the secretary? Maybe books don't count."

But Gale wouldn't give up, so doggedly they continued through every book. Not a sign of any secret. Then book by book they had to fill the shelves again and lock the glass doors.

"Next the drawers," Gale said. They pulled out the bottom drawer first—empty. Together they pulled out the sticky middle one—empty, too. The top drawer was rounded and had no handles, but gripping it together, they tugged it forward and halfway out. It was filled with heaps of old writing paper mixed with old envelopes and blotters. No sign of any secret recipe for a happy life.

But catching hold of the two sides to pull it farther out, Lucy by chance touched a small button on either side, and the whole front of the drawer came down flat.

"Look, Gale, this way it's a desk!" exclaimed Lucy.

"Nobody ever uses it for a desk. I'd know if they did," Gale said. "I come here every single summer."

"It is a desk, anyway," Lucy said, as she eased the flat surface as far out as she could. "Look, the back has cubbyholes and two little drawers."

"All the cubbyholes are empty, though," Gale said. They both peered in. "How about those tiny drawers?" He slid open the one on his side with no trouble, but it was as empty as the cubbyholes.

"Mine won't budge," Lucy told him as she tugged on hers. "Something's stuck."

"Wait till I get a paring knife from the kitchen." In no time he was back with one. While Lucy jiggled the drawer and slightly pushed it to and fro, he slipped the knife around the top of it. Suddenly the paper that had been holding it back let go. Onto the floor fell the drawer and its load of old papers—yellowed programs and announcements and advertisements for concerts and lectures.

But in the space behind the drawer was a page of a very old newspaper, obviously stuck there for many, many years. At the top, half torn away, was part of the paper's name, so it read *nal Aegis*. "Might be *National*, if it was all there, but the date's clear, Gale. It says September 20, 1820. That's almost 100 years old! A whole century, Gale!"

Lucy might be impressed, but Gale wasn't. "Uh-huh," he said. "But what's the secret?"

Lucy turned the page. "Look, here's something checked with a pencil. 'Married—in this town, on Thurfday evening laft, by Rev. Mr. Going, Mr. Daniel Goddard to Mifs Sally Whitney, daughter of Mr. Ifrael Whitney.' Sounds funny with all that 'Thurfday evening laft' and 'Mifs' and 'Ifrael,' but that's Grandfather Gale's grandmother and grandfather. I know they lived to have a golden wedding anniversary, so—"

Gale interrupted her. "You mean we did all this to find out we have to get married to have a happy life? Not much use to you and me, is it?" he asked sourly.

"Well, I'm not exactly thrilled either," Lucy admitted. "That was the grandmother who said the recipe was in the secretary, so I suppose to her—" Lucy was slowly folding the page as she talked.

Then—in italics, at the top of the same column, were the four words: *Leave no ftone unturned*.

"I've got it, Gale, I've got it!" Lucy almost squealed, as she handed the page to Gale.

"Leave no ftone unturned," Gale read out loud. "What in the dickens is a *ftone*, Lucy?" he asked.

"It's the old spelling for *stone*, that's all. And that's the motto of my club in Wales, so it must mean the motto is right for me and so is Wales," Lucy explained.

Gale was not excited in the least, and she couldn't blame him. "Okay, you'll find a happy life in Wales, but what about me?" he grumbled, as they began putting everything but the newspaper back in the drawer.

"I know what about you," Lucy said. "I heard my father talking last night to your mother, and he wants you to come to Wales next summer. He said it would be good for you to camp on the Pembina River and belong to the Cave Men."

Gale began to grin. "Sounds like a recipe for a happy life. I'll leave no ftone unturned!"

Late in the afternoon, Father and the three boys came in, all sweaty and fishy. "Quick, now—all of us off to the bathhouse and into the lake before the women come home," Father said. "Want to come, Lucy and Gale?"

As they all ran across the lawn toward the lake, Lucy

again admired the screened lookout, with its view of the broad lake and its hammocks and cushioned chairs. She couldn't imagine anything more different from Wales. The lookout was at the top of a little tower, built against the steep bank. The floor beneath it was a bathhouse, with four small changing rooms, where you hung up your clothes and later left your wet sandy bathing suit. Under that was the boathouse, empty now of all but one rowboat and several pairs of oars.

They were all in the water when the five women came home, very hot looking in their dusters and dresses. Cousin Frances was into her bathing suit and ruffled rubber cap in no time, but Minerva sat in a hammock reading a book until dinnertime. To Lucy, Minerva was a riddle. She was tall and very serious and yet not entirely grown up, with her dark hair down her back. She smiled sweetly, but she seldom said much. Lucy heard someone say, "Minerva's so bright that she's going to Vassar."

Mother later explained that Vassar was a girls' college in the East. Since this sounded interesting, Lucy asked Father that night as he stood looking over books on a table, "Will I go to Vassar, like Minerva?"

"Indeed and you will not go to any girls' college in the East," he answered her sharply. "You and Amory are growing up in North Dakota, and you'll go to your own state university. And mind, Lucy," he continued rather severely, "don't you let this trip put ideas in your head."

This was an odd answer, since she'd asked him because she didn't have any idea at all. Away from Wales, even Father was hard to understand.

And Lucy said to herself, "If Father does come back to be a professor in the city, will we all change?"

The Biggest
Circus in the World

On Friday Mother went to a concert in the city, so
Aunt Lucy arranged a shoe-shopping trip in the nearby
town of Excelsior. Grandfather insisted on going along.
"I want to be sure Lucy gets a stout pair of shoes," he
said.

The pair he finally chose for her were so stout that
the soles didn't bend. And Lucy clomped around the
store, trying to be pleased but really feeling that she
might as well be wearing Dutch wooden shoes.

Aunt Lucy solved that problem also. "Those shoes
will be fine at home," she said to Lucy. "But you're my
namesake so nobody can scold us if I buy you two more
pairs. Try on those low tan shoes and that pair of patent
leather slippers."

Three new pairs of shoes at once so amazed Lucy that

at first she didn't even say thank-you. But Aunt Lucy must have understood, for she leaned over and kissed Lucy, saying, "And now you can lose a shoe in every mudhole on the drive home and perhaps have two left."

That evening while the grown-ups talked, Lucy sat beside the secretary, dreaming of the next day's circus. At the same time she thought of the secret in the secretary and wondered if she'd left no stone unturned. Should she try to deliver Luke's message to Toby Shaw right at the circus? "It's my last chance," she said to herself. She quietly opened the top drawer of the secretary, took out a piece of paper and an envelope, and went upstairs.

On the dresser was Father's fountain pen. Ink would look more important than pencil. Quickly she wrote, "Dear Mr. Toby Shaw, I hope you're in Canada, but if you aren't, please go. Luke wants you." She signed it, "A friend of Luke Morgan."

Then she folded it, sealed it in the envelope, and wrote "Mr. Toby Shaw, Care of the Bradna Dogs" on the outside. That address didn't suit her, but it was all she knew. Next she faced the problem of delivering a letter to a dog trainer in a circus where hundreds of people worked. She could never manage such an errand alone, and the only one who could was Grandfather.

The next morning, right after breakfast, she took her envelope and followed Grandfather out to his garden, where he was picking lettuce for the dinner salad. "Want to stay home from the circus and weed my garden?" he joked.

"Not really, Grandfather." Lucy laughed. Then she asked, "Do you think you could help me deliver a letter to a man that works in the circus?" She paused and then added, "And I have to keep it secret."

"Secret letters already!" Grandfather exclaimed. "Or is it from someone in Wales that doesn't want anybody to know about this?"

To that last question, Lucy could honestly answer, "Yes, that's it. And do you think you can help me?" she went on.

"Well, hand it over and I'll see," he said. As he took the letter from her, he asked one more question. "Have you any idea what's in this?"

"Oh, yes. It's nothing bad," Lucy said. And she ran back to the house before he could ask her anything more.

For the circus, Lucy wore her new patent leather slippers, and all the cousins wore their best clothes. Even Amory had on a necktie, which he kept loosening and allowing to hang under one ear, until Mother or one of the aunts reminded him, "Amory, your tie's loose again. Tighten it up."

"Gee whiz, if they want to strangle me, why don't they just put a noose around my neck and hang me?" he complained to Father.

But Father had no sympathy for him. "This once, Amory, you dress as the city expects you to dress. And that's that."

All the grown-ups were going to the city on errands or to see old friends. Only Grandfather and Joe and the seven cousins were going to the circus, first having their lunch with Uncle Albert's mother, whom everyone called Grandma Turnbull.

When it was time to go, Grandfather sat in front with Joe and held Gale on his lap. That left six cousins for the backseat and the two little folding seats, which had no springs and faced backward. Amory and Robert immediately decided those jump seats were for "the little ones," Albert and Lucy. The big boys also decided the girls should squeeze those fancy skirts together and make room for a boy on each side, on the outside, the view side, of course.

Since neither Minerva nor Frances was ready for battle, Amory and Robert took the best places, and Lucy and Albert jounced along on the hard little seats, seeing everything after they'd passed it. Lucy had never ridden this way before, and everything she saw seemed already secondhand.

But it was the city, and city was what she had come to see. The paved streets, the trees on either side, the shrubs and the lawns, the rows and rows of houses—no wonder Gwin said she hadn't seen anything when she'd seen only Wales. Since Joe drove much faster than Father ever did, they were soon parked in front of a big cream-colored brick house.

Amory and Robert opened their doors, ran to the porch, and pushed the doorbell before anyone else was unfolded and upright. As Lucy came to the top of the front steps, the door opened and a maid in a pink dress with a white organdy apron and a little ruffled headband stood waiting for them to come in.

And they entered the big hallway, where the cousins were all kissed by a very small old lady, Grandma Turnbull.

"Lunch is waiting," she said. "But first, all go upstairs to wash." Up the wide carpeted stairs and along a hall, Lucy went with the girls, and then into the most imposing bathroom in the world, Lucy was sure. It was all tile, shiny taps, and rows of towels with initials embroidered on them, everything so different from the kitchen basin and the roller towel at home, and so magnificent that Lucy barely dampened her fingers and dried them on one corner of the smallest towel.

Downstairs, they went into the long dining room, and the maid passed chicken salad and hot rolls that were wrapped in a linen napkin. Everyone, even Amory, spoke in subdued voices, and Lucy spoke not at all, except to answer Grandma Turnbull's question of how old she was. And when Grandma Turnbull heard she was nearly eleven, she said, "Why I thought children grew very big in the country. Now Lucy, you must have a second helping." So Lucy had to have a second plateful of salad before she could set to work on the big glass dish of chocolate ice cream running with chocolate sauce and topped with nuts.

Grandfather pulled out his pocket watch as the boys began their second dishes of ice cream, but they ate so efficiently that their dishes were empty before he could warn them to hurry.

"Into the sitting room for a minute to get your chocolate Ting-lings," Grandma Turnbull ordered.

While Lucy was munching her Ting-ling, she looked out the window and saw a girl about her age with a terrier on a leash. Topsy didn't have a leash, and probably no dog in Cavalier County had one either. And this dog's collar was such a bright red leather that Lucy wondered if the dog was a special rare breed. So she called to Grandma Turnbull, "Would you know what kind of dog that is? Or what its name is?"

"I've no idea," Grandma Turnbull answered. "The girl belongs to a family that moved into our block a few months ago, and I don't know her name either. People come and go. That's the way it is in a city, Lucy," she explained.

"I'm glad it's not that way in Wales," Lucy said to herself, as she thought of what might have happened to the Dickermans if they'd lived in a city instead of a village. Where would Hilda have run for help? But then, the doctor? It was all very mixed up. Maybe in a city you found a doctor, but in a village you found friends.

Soon they took off for the circus grounds, and before long they were standing at the gate. Grandfather showed his tickets and in they went to the hot dusty grounds with thousands of other people.

Ahead of them was a vast tent, a tent of such size and such height that Lucy again paused, just to stare.

"Come, Lucy," said Grandfather, pulling her along rather impatiently. "It's a long walk past the sideshows, and we don't want to miss the parade of the whole company around all three rings. Just wait till you see that!" Grandfather was as excited as the boys.

"How about just one sideshow," asked Robert.

"Haven't time," Grandfather said. "All of you look at the painted signs and listen to the barkers as we go by."

So they straggled past the sideshows, Grandfather and the big girls calling to the boys to hurry, and Lucy trying to see and hear everything without letting go of Grandfather's hand.

Besides the fortune-teller and the skeleton man and the fat woman, there were a bearded lady and a blue man. They puzzled Cousin Frances especially, but Lucy was able to quote her Cousin Len. "Probably something wrong with their chemistry."

Amory and Robert slowed down to hear about the sword-swallowers and the fire-eaters, but Grandfather, using his loudest voice, called out, "Boys! You can eat nearly everything, but swords and fire are out of your class. Come along!"

Then Robert stopped to hear the whole rigmarole about the hard-headed man. "You can hit him with a sledgehammer and he doesn't care!" shouted the barker.

This time Albert yelled back. "Hey, Robert, come on! I bet if I hit you on the head with a sledgehammer, you wouldn't care either!"

By that time they were all walking faster and faster, and finally they entered the enormous tent, passed along the tiers of seats and settled in their places. Lucy had barely time to crane her neck for a look at the top of the tent, to twist around once to gaze at the thousands of people, and to look down at her beautiful shiny shoes, now gray with dust, before two brass bands in scarlet uniforms came marching in, and behind them the parade.

In her wildest daydreams, Lucy had never imagined such a procession of prancing horses and glittering costumes, of satin and silk and spangles, of gilded coaches and chariots, of camels and elephants, broken-down autos for the clowns, and a beautiful long limousine for someone who must be king of the circus.

Grandfather nudged her. "Didn't I tell you? Didn't I tell you?" he kept saying.

Before she knew where they came from, the air was full of acrobats, the elephants were doing tricks in one ring, the seals in another, and overhead a woman was waltzing on a tightrope so high under the tent roof that Lucy knew before Amory leaned across Grandfather to remind her, "Those nets underneath aren't that much help, you know. If she falls into them the wrong way, she breaks her neck—snap! Quick as that!"

The only trouble was, Lucy discovered, that she was not a three-ring person. As soon as she fixed her eyes on one ring, one of the boys shouted, "Hey, look at that!" And when she looked, Grandfather or Frances poked her in the ribs and said, "Look! You're missing something." Then when she was staring at that act, they'd poke her again, "Lucy, over there—quick, or you'll miss it!"

She grew pop-eyed from looking, but she missed the first or the last part of every act, so that it seemed to her that the acrobats were left in midair, the elephants were frozen with one leg up, and the balls bounced into the air off the seals' noses and never came down.

The vendors of candy and pop and ice-cream cones arrived regularly at their row of seats. All the cousins had spending money, and once while they were carefully choosing their cones, Lucy saw Grandfather slip her envelope and some coins into the vendor's hand. And she heard him say, "Think you can get this to the man it should go to?"

"Sure can," the vendor answered. "I've got to stock up again soon. I'll take it out back then." And after that, Lucy watched him along the rows until he finally disappeared.

Another vendor soon came along, selling boxes of Cracker Jack. Now Amory, with a great flourish, opened his new wallet and drew out his dollar bill. "The Cracker Jack is my treat," he said. "And I'll bet we all get good prizes in it. I'm always lucky on Cracker Jack boxes."

Lucy opened her box, and right on top was a girl's ring with a colored stone. That was luck! But the four boys each got a girl's ring too, and that wasn't their idea of luck.

But Amory always found a way to make a good impression. "Let's give all of them to Lucy," he suggested. "She's got a club at home called the Stone Age Girls, and I bet they'd like these." Maybe he did it just

for show, but Lucy was grateful just the same.

Right after that, into the middle ring came a dozen white horses, with a gorgeous woman and a tall man entirely clothed in white satin. And after them ran a troop of white dogs. Lucy knew at once that these were the Bradna dogs, the best dog act in the world.

She could see that Topsy's waltzing wasn't much. But then Topsy didn't have a mistress who stood on two galloping white horses at one time. And Topsy wouldn't even recognize her mistress if she wore that slinky white satin outfit with white elbow-length kid gloves and carried that white ostrich-plume fan.

These dogs jumped through impossible hoops, danced alone and in pairs, pushed doll carriages and sat at tables, barked the right answers to arithmetic problems, and one even knelt to say its prayers. As she watched all this, she thought of Toby Shaw, and she hoped he was with Luke and not in the circus lot behind the tent. And she thought of the sideshow boy, and she hoped that some day he could leave that mean little sideshow and come back to the Bradna dogs.

The boys had paid no attention to the horses or dogs. They were counting the number of twists the girl with the iron jaw made around the rope at the tent top. Lucy never heard their final score, but she did hear Robert's comment. "Wouldn't you know an iron jaw would belong to a girl? Bet she can talk—and how!"

Before the girls could answer, a band played "Dixie." At once the Turnbull cousins began pushing Albert to his feet. Lucy was puzzled, not by "Dixie," which was on that famous player piano roll at school, but by their insisting that Albert should stand. Why only Albert? They all shoved and hauled at him until he did stand up for the last few bars of "Dixie," one lone boy in a white suit standing among the thousands sitting there.

"Why must Albert stand, all alone?" Lucy whispered to Frances.

"He's the only one of us born in Virginia, so he belongs to the South," Frances replied. Lucy felt sorry for him, with all those pairs of eyes staring at him. Being born in Wales, North Dakota, seemed far, far better.

At the end of the circus came the chariot race. Lucy told herself, "They run this race two times every day, so they must know what they're doing." But they grew more and more reckless it seemed to her, so she half-squinted and only pretended to watch.

But she was watching enough to see the ice-cream vendor come up to Grandfather and speak directly in his ear. Grandfather nodded. And when the race was over and they were standing up to leave, Grandfather half whispered into her ear, "That young man's not here. Gone home to Canada, they say. They'll forward his mail." Lucy nodded, and she smiled her widest grin, what Amory called her jack-o'-lantern grin.

On the drive back to the lake, she sat so quiet on her jump seat that Grandfather turned around and asked, "You there, Lucy? I hear everyone but you. What did you like best of all?"

"The thirty white dogs, Grandfather," Lucy answered, and then realized no one else would agree.

Even Grandfather exploded. "I take you to the greatest show on earth, and you like thirty white dogs best of all? Jumping Jehosophat! What a girl!"

Back at the lake cottage, the family was beginning dinner when the circus crew arrived. Lucy took one look at the table of food and knew she'd be sick if she added a single morsel to Grandma Turnbull's lunch and the circus vendors' pop and candy and cones and Cracker Jack.

So she asked Mother, "Could I skip dinner?"

Unluckily, Aunt Frances heard her, and suggested, "Better take the child's temperature, Caroline." But Mother answered, "Nonsense! She's just got circus stomach." And she led Lucy upstairs.

"Where's Father?" Lucy asked as Mother tucked her into the cot.

"Today he went to the university," Mother said. "Remember?"

Late that night Lucy woke to hear Father talking in the bed beside her, "Helmuth's gone home to Germany, so they want me to come back."

"Yes?" Mother said softly.

"It's summer session, but the crowds, Caroline. While I listened about courses, I looked out the window at the street with all that traffic, and my head began to ache— the way it used to." He paused, and Mother said nothing. "I should have waited and asked you about it, but I just told him *no*. I can't come back to the university or to city life, Caroline. I can't." And Father stopped talking.

"I understand," Mother answered gently.

"Wales and the prairie have been good for me," Father went on, "but for you—"

"Don't you worry about me, Harry," Mother said. "You're well there, and we have a good life."

Lucy must have dozed off at once, for she heard nothing more.

The next morning, as Mother brushed Lucy's hair, she said, "Because you already know something about it, I'm telling you, Lucy, but don't you tell anyone else. We've had a chance to move to the city, but we're going back to Wales—for good."

Dozens of Cousins

Downstairs at breakfast, Grandfather's blessing was longer than usual, both because it was Sunday and because in three days the whole family would scatter again. Lucy loved the breakfasts at the lake house the best of any meals—no oatmeal, but special hot breads, and copper finger bowls to dabble in when you'd finished your fruit.

Amory paid slight attention to his finger bowl. He was already full of plans. "Grandfather, an article in the *Minneapolis Journal* said the circus people fish all day today at Deep Haven. How about it? Couldn't we fish there today too?"

Robert must have been planning also, for he immediately chimed in. "We could see the blue man for free, and the strong man that can lift a horse, and one of the midgets might fall in and we could—"

"Whoa!" Grandfather finally got in a word. "Have you boys forgotten this is Sunday? Circus people may have no other day to fish, but for the rest of us—no fishing on Sunday."

Aunt Lucy changed the subject by asking Grandfather about the next day's big Gale reunion on Gale Island. "It's the first time all three generations of us have gone, isn't it?"

Though Lucy knew of this annual reunion, she had tried not to think about it. It would be a picnic with dozens of strangers, all relatives, but not close relatives like real cousins. Somehow Amory and the boys would have a good time, but she knew she'd be glad when it was over.

At the end of the meal, Grandfather put his hand in the pocket of his black alpaca jacket and then looked very astonished. "Well, well, well," he said and pulled out two envelopes. "Mail forwarded to you from Wales, Harry. I clean forgot it last night." And he gave it to Lucy to take to Father at the other end of the table.

Though Lucy held the two envelopes only a minute, she saw that one had a Canadian stamp, like the ones she had seen on the Owens' mail. So she couldn't resist asking Mother, "Couldn't that Canadian letter be from Mrs. Owen? They're back in Canada by now."

"Writing your father instead of me? Don't be silly. Anyway, there's not time for her to have written to Wales and have it forwarded here," Mother answered, as they followed Father up to the bedroom.

There he first opened the letter from the bank, reading most of it aloud to Mother. "A small hailstorm, no big losses, mostly good weather—that loan to the Dormuths—hmmmmmmm," and he mumbled on, with

Mother listening but Lucy paying little attention.

Then he held up the letter he'd now taken from the Canadian envelope, and onto the floor fell a one-dollar bill. "Look," Father said, "here's a letter from Luke Morgan. I never thought I'd hear from him again. Why he's already in Winnipeg, and he's joined the army, but he says, 'It's not so bad because my best friend joined when I did. That helps.' "

"Just what I hoped!" Lucy exclaimed before she could stop herself.

"What do you mean? 'Just what you hoped'?" asked Father, looking up from the letter and staring at her. Then he went on reading the rest of the letter. "Listen, Caroline, to what he writes. 'Thanks for loaning me books and magazines when I was at my uncle's. And thanks for telling me to come back to Canada. I don't think I could have made it without you and your family. I heard you've got a boy and a girl, and maybe they could split this dollar and get something kids like. Yours truly, Luke Morgan.' "

"What a nice young man," Mother said. "Pity he was the one caught in that useless raid. And since he's an orphan, it's good he's got his best friend with him, isn't it?"

"Uh-huh," said Father, apparently thinking of something else. "Lucy, I've promised to take the boys rowing this morning since they can't fish, but late this afternoon, why don't you and I go for a row, alone?"

"I'd love it," Lucy answered.

So late that afternoon, when the sun wasn't as hot as it had been, Father rowed off with Lucy, telling Amory, who wanted to come along, that he had a date with Lucy.

Out from the shore, Father lifted the oars up and sat

listening. "Listen to that lonely loon," he said. And faintly, from far across the lake, came the loon's call again, though if Father hadn't heard the first call, she'd have missed them both.

"Now, while we're waiting for another loon to call, tell me, Lucy, how much do you know about Luke Morgan? How did you happen to hope he had his friend with him? Did you ever even see Luke Morgan?" And Father sat waiting for the answers.

So Lucy began, as far back as the raid on the blind pig when she had taken the forbidden shortcut, and told about her feeding Luke and hiding him in the cave until he could escape to Canada. She included the message she had tried to deliver to Toby Shaw and the jack-knife missing from the cave, and she even confessed how she had learned about bedbugs.

Father listened without asking a single question until she was all done. Then he said, "So you thought he was a transient, yet you weren't afraid when he stood at the door of the stone house and you were home alone."

"He didn't look like a bad transient. Just a lost one." Then she asked Father a question. "Would you say Luke was a convict that I helped to escape?"

"You could call him that if you want to sound fancy," Father said, laughing. "Maybe you could call him a jailbird, but not a convict. He hadn't been convicted of anything." Then Father closed the whole matter with a warning. "Talk to me any time you like about this, but your mother will worry about you and the transients that go past our house if she knows. So at least until winter comes, keep it a secret for you and me."

He dipped the oars in the water again and rowed them quickly back to shore, Lucy guiding him by the peak of the lookout. She was immensely relieved that to Father at least she'd no longer have to make up fibs about Luke.

At dinner, Grandfather and Aunt Frances tried to give all the news of all the relatives they'd see at the picnic. But Lucy was soon lost among Cousin Anna and Cousin Isobel and Cousin Alice and Cousin Percy. And when she discovered these were only the older folks and only a few of them, she gave up. She longed for a picnic back home on the Pembina River, and not this gathering of unknown distant cousins.

On Monday morning they drove to a dock where a launch took them to Gale Island. That part of the picnic Lucy liked, for she'd never been on the water in anything but a rowboat before.

Amory hung so far over the side that Mother looked the other way. When Robert and Albert leaned quite as far over, Aunt Lucy spoke. "Boys, sit up. That's no way to behave in a launch." And the boys did sit up, even Amory, who looked surprised. Father hadn't said anything. Where Amory was concerned, Father always held his thunder for the big events. If Amory wasn't about to be killed or about to kill someone, Father let him be.

Once on the island there were even more relatives than Lucy had imagined. Everyone made a great fuss over Mother and her sisters and Minerva and Frances, but no one seemed to know what to say to Lucy. Mostly they asked her how old she was, and when she said she was nearly eleven, they usually answered, "My, you are small for your age, aren't you?" And after that, there wasn't much more to say.

One big girl about Minerva's age came up and tried to make Lucy feel at home. "You must be Carrie Gale's little girl, come all the way from that village near

Canada," she began.

"Yes, I'm from Wales, North Dakota," Lucy answered bluntly, but she had no idea what to say next.

"And is it a pretty little town?" asked the good-natured girl. "Do nice things happen when you live way off in the country like that, away from the noise and dirt of a city?"

"Oh, yes—well, sometimes—oh, no," Lucy said. "Some things are nice. I've got three new friends and a dog that can do tricks. But no, I don't think it's really a nice, pretty little town." Lucy felt she should be truthful. "Some people say it's rough and wicked."

"Wicked!" The tall girl started to laugh. "What could be wicked about a tiny bit of a village way off there?" But before Lucy could give her any facts about the wickedness, someone called the girl and off she went to the big house on the island.

By now dozens of relatives were all over the lawn and on the porch and sitting on the swings and standing by the picnic tables. But Lucy felt alone, as though she was somewhere she didn't belong. Mother was indoors with a very old invalid aunt. Amory had gone off with Robert and Albert, and Aunt Frances was taking Gale around to greet all the relatives.

To avoid being asked anymore questions about her age or about Wales, Lucy went down a path between untrimmed bushes to the sandy shore of the lake. There, sitting on a rock, with his coat and tie off and shirt-sleeves rolled up, was Father, chewing on a stalk of sweet grass.

"Father, why—" Lucy started to ask.

"Shhh," he put his finger to his lips. "There's a heron fishing off there," he whispered. "Come down by me where you can watch." After she sat down beside him,

Father continued to whisper. "A few minutes ago there was a bittern here. It flew off, but I'd heard its call. That's what led me here."

Then he looked away from the fishing heron and at Lucy. "What led you here, my dear?" he asked.

"I'm not at home with all those cousins," she whispered back. "Are you, Father?"

"They're nice, and they're one reason your mother so much wanted to come," he answered. "But maybe you and I are more at home—"

"In Wales?" said Lucy so loud that the heron lifted his wide wings and flapped away.

"Yes, I suppose in Wales," Father echoed her, "where I have the prairie and the farmers I do business with. And you have Topsy and the Owens—and now and then an escaped convict," he teased, as he stood up to go back to the reunion picnic.

The day after the picnic was Tuesday, the last day the family would be all together at the lake. The Turnbull cousins were moving to Grandma Turnbull's house for the rest of their stay, and Wednesday was the latest the Johnstons could leave for their four-day drive home.

The boys had gone off, telling Lucy she couldn't go along. Upstairs Mother had begun to pack. In the kitchen Christine was busy on a celebration dinner. Aunt Lucy and the girls were shut in their rooms, packing the seven suitcases that were made to order to fit the made-to-order trunks that were fastened to the Packard. Grandfather invited Lucy to weed lettuce with him, but she wasn't going to spoil her last day by weeding. She could do that at home.

"I'm bored, that's what I am," she said to herself. "Imagine being bored in a big house on a lake." And she remembered that Father thought that was why Mrs.

Bortz had eloped. Though she wasn't sure about elop-
ing, she did see how you could be bored in a mansion,
and perhaps if a handsome man—

She daydreamed a moment, and then she drifted out
to the porch. At once she knew she wasn't wanted.
Father was with Aunt Frances, who looked rather
weepy. "You're right to take a job, Frances, and one in
a settlement house in a slum should help you forget—"
Father looked up and saw Lucy, who was trying to back
through the door.

"Lucy, here's the new guidebook I bought in the
city," he called out. "Why don't you go somewhere and
look at it?" She knew very well he was trying to get rid
of her.

She reached for the book and scurried away. This
house had too many porches and rooms and halls, she
decided. At home, she always knew where everyone
was and where she wasn't wanted. Having nothing else
to read, she spent the rest of the morning on the guidebook, planning a new route back to Wales. Every trail
now had a beautiful name—The National Parks Trans-
continental Highway, the Minnesota Scenic Highway,
and the Daniel Boone Trail. She could hardly wait to
spring those names on Amory.

Shortly before lunch, the four boys came in, all so
dirty that each mother grabbed her son before he
arrived at the table. Aunt Frances gave Gale an entire
quick bath, and he changed everything. Aunt Lucy
simply said to Robert and Albert, "Go clean up. Be
spick-and-span in ten minutes," and she didn't sound
cross, only very definite. Mother looked at Amory with
his knickers torn at one knee and his black stocking
torn at the other, and his blue shirt streaked with dust.
"Well, your hair's clean," Mother said. "Work from

there on down."

At lunch Father made the mistake of turning to the small table and asking, "Where did you boys go to get so grimy?"

The other boys left it to Amory to answer, since it was his father who asked. "We've been all over, and we've climbed on the window ledges and we've looked in the cracks and we've poked at the rafters of every single outhouse," Amory explained.

"Outhouse?" Minerva asked in a rather shocked voice. "What do you mean?"

"Robert said that if you kill a spider, the next day it rains," Amory went on. "And if it rains, nobody can leave tomorrow. And Albert thought spiders lived mostly in outhouses, but I always thought an outhouse was a privy, and—"

"Hush at the table," interrupted Aunt Frances.

"Anyway, Robert said any shed might have spiders, so it didn't have to be a—" Amory looked around the table, "a you-know-what. And Gale was right. None of the houses here have a—" Amory paused again, "a you-know-what, so Robert—"

"Robert can tell me after lunch," Aunt Lucy broke in.

Lucy began to get the giggles. Amory was obviously too much for these aunts. And Father's cheeks were puffed out, as they always were when he was trying to keep from laughing, and Cousin Frances had her napkin up to her face, but right through the napkin you could hear her giggles.

"In Wales, of course, an outhouse is always a you-know-what, but I suppose—" Amory was wound up, and it took Mother to halt him.

"Amory Johnston! You keep still!" Mother commanded.

And for a moment Amory did keep still, but he always had to have the last word. "We never found a single spider. At home we could have found dozens of them, I know we could, especially out in the—well, you know what." He ended in a low voice, and everyone thought he was done. But not Amory. He looked up and smiled his best smile. "Wales is ab-so-lute-ly crawling with spiders!"

Father broke into a loud guffaw. "All right, Amory," he said, "that's a score for Wales. Now let's forget spiders and plan the bonfire for tonight."

Late in the afternoon, Father took Gale and Lucy for a last row, and as they came up the stairs from the boathouse, they heard Mother screaming, "Amory Johnston! You almost shot me! And what are you doing with your BB gun anyway?"

Father ran up the last steps, Lucy and Gale right behind him. There was Mother snatching the BB gun from Amory. She was red as a beet and furiously angry. Amory was already at work, explaining.

"You know Uncle Albert came back and we didn't expect him, and I just thought I'd shoot the gun to celebrate—you know, like a royal salute. And how was I to guess you'd be skulking under those thick trees?"

Mother now had the gun, and for a moment it looked as though she might fire it at Amory. "Skulking! I was taking a farewell walk under my father's shade trees. Skulking, indeed!" Mother glared, and Amory tried a smile. But it was a very feeble smile.

Then Father took the gun and emptied it right there of every single BB. Amory looked on mournfully as one by one his shots tumbled to the ground. The empty gun was wrapped in a piece of canvas, and Mother went with Father to be sure it was securely strapped on the packed suitcases on the Regal trunk rack. Amory, for once, said nothing at all.

There was a last evening of watching the twilight on the lake and a last candlelit dinner. Then Father managed the bonfire at the back of the garden lot. Everyone toasted marshmallows and offered them, sticky brown or charred black, to everyone else. And Lucy seeing them all together now, as she had that first evening, felt Mother was right when she had once said, "Amory and Lucy may not have some things, but they're rich in cousins." She was rich in cousins—nice ones. She wished suddenly that they could all come to Wales. She had a feeling they'd like it, at least for a visit.

They were leaving so early in the morning that Father insisted all good-byes should be said that night. By the time they went up to bed, there had been so many kisses and hugs that Lucy felt completely squeezed out of shape.

As Lucy was dropping off to sleep in her folks' room, she heard Father say, "Has it been as good as you dreamed, Caroline?"

"In some ways even better, Harry," Mother answered. "But now I'm anxious to get home."

"And so am I," Lucy said to herself.

"Dear Old Wales!"

Very early on Wednesday, Mother leaned over Lucy's cot and said, "Get up quietly, Lucy. Don't make any noise. Only Aunt Frances and Christine are up, getting us some breakfast, and then we leave."

Down in the kitchen the four of them quickly and quietly ate. Then Father carried down the last bag, and they were warming up the Regal when the whole cottage erupted. Everyone was in robe and slippers and no one was fully awake, but everyone was there in a row at the back door. Grandfather stood by Aunt Frances and Gale, and Uncle Albert was there with Aunt Lucy and their tall children. In the dim, misty early morning light, they all called, "Good-bye! Good-bye!" and waved and threw kisses—well, none of the boys threw kisses, but the women did.

Finally they were all out of sight, around the curve. And for several miles, the Regal made the only noise on the road. No other autos were out, the day had not really begun, and everyone was too sleepy to say more than, "There's the Green Trail mark," or "The book says 'Creamery on the right,' but how do we know it's a creamery when it hasn't got a sign?"

At noon they stopped to eat the lunch Christine had made, and while they stood under a clump of trees, Father said, "What about our taking a different route to Fargo? Only Lucy and I have read the new guide-book, but you can take my word for it. If we turn north, we'll hit the Scenic Highway. How does that sound?"

"Let me see that guidebook," said Amory, almost grabbing it from Father. And he began to read off the trail names. "How about Canada, Kansas City and Gulf Highway? I like that! And there's a King of Trails, and listen to this one—the Chippewa Trail. Let's do that one, and when I get home I could say—"

"Wait a minute, Amory," Father laughed. "You've picked the flossiest names, but they all begin at the Twin Cities and go out of the state in the wrong direction." Then he said to Lucy, "What trail did you pick —going toward home, if you please?"

Lucy was ready with an answer. "I noticed the Black Diamond trail goes right through Detroit Lakes, where you were born, Father. We haven't even seen it."

Father looked pleased. "Imagine—there's a trail there now. And when my father went there from Boston, he had to help cut the timber to start the town." He turned to Mother. "How about it, Caroline?"

"If you like, Harry, but I kept that log to go back on the Green Trail and then the Red." Mother wasn't enthusiastic, but she agreed.

So after a while they turned north, or at least they thought they turned north, to go through Alexandria and Detroit Lakes. But the sun had gone under a cloud and the new guidebook was in tenths of miles, which confused Amory.

Finally Father said, "Amory are you sure we're on the right trail? I haven't seen a mark of any kind for miles."

"In seven-tenths of a mile we'll pass a cemetery on our right," Amory answered. "You'd think a cemetery would stay put, wouldn't you?" Amory leaned over to check the speedometer. "Take a look! That speedometer's broken. Been broken for the last—well, I don't know for how long." Amory sounded upset.

"Here's another auto coming toward us," Mother said. "This once, Harry, do ask someone where we are," she begged. Father never liked to ask anyone directions. He always said if he waited long enough he'd find out for himself.

Before the two autos met, the Regal began to jerk and bump. "Rats! Another flat! Rats! Rats!" Father drew up at the side of the road, the man drove by, and Mother said nothing.

While they stood for the next half hour, either helping Father or carefully staying out of his way, no one mentioned their being lost. But lost they certainly were. Then when the tire was fixed and Father was cranking the Regal, a bright red auto came toward them. This time Mother stood boldly out in the road and waved her handkerchief.

The auto slowed down beside the Regal. And the driver was a woman, all by herself. Mother was so astonished that for a moment she said nothing. Then she asked, "Could you tell us where we are? And where this road goes?"

"You're on the way to Minneapolis. I know you'll love it. I've just been there," the woman replied gaily.

Mother was speechless. So it was Lucy who spoke up. "We've just been there too, and we love it, but we want to leave it now."

"Turn around then and go in the opposite direction," the woman called, shifted her gears with a screech, waved, and was gone.

After the Regal was turned around and they were driving back on the road they had come, Father cleared his throat with a Harumph! "Perhaps you're right, Caroline," he said. "We'll follow your log and the Green Trail back through Willmar and Benson and Morris, the way we came."

Then in one of his sudden shifts of mood, Father exclaimed, "I almost forgot that Canadian dollar bill Luke Morgan sent for you children! Remember that good little variety store we saw in Morris? Tomorrow we'll stop there a few minutes and you can shop for bargains."

Mother dozed in the backseat, while Amory and Lucy argued about what they'd buy. Amory wanted a jack-knife for Jerry and one for Stan, but Lucy's choice of barrettes for herself and the Owen girls and Hilda, he called, "Dopey, real dopey." So he began planning how she should spend her share. "How about water pistols, Lucy? There's lots of times you might want water pistols. Or if you girls didn't want them all the time, I bet we boys could use them."

Lucy stuck to her barrettes. "Luke Morgan would want me to spend that money as I please, Amory. I know he would—I know it!" But she didn't tell Amory how she knew it.

Though it made a very long day's drive, with all that

to-and-froing in the wrong direction and the flat tire, they kept on after dark to reach the Benson hotel. Everything was as good as the time before, "Plus my having six shoes now instead of only one," Lucy said to herself.

In Morris the next day, Father shooed them into the variety store, saying, "Be quick about it." They swiftly picked out the knives and barrettes and were on the way to the door, when Father said, "Lucy, you never have much extra cash to spend. What else do you see that you'd like? We can spare five minutes more," he said, "and I'll foot the bill."

Lucy scanned the counters and the shelves, and in less than five minutes she had chosen. "That little tan cardboard satchel would hold Clarissa's things, and Topsy would love that narrow red collar, and Baby Charlie should have that blue celluloid rattle. But that all comes to seventy-five cents beyond my fifty for barrettes."

"Here," said Father, as he put three quarters in her hand, "I'm sure Luke Morgan would say you'd earned it, and I think so too."

Later while the speedometer was being repaired in a real garage in Breckenridge, Father put through a long-distance call to Moorhead. Gwen answered the phone at the Maclarens', and Lucy heard her say, "Early to-morrow morning? I can't wait!"

"I can't wait either!" Lucy exclaimed to Father.

"You'll have to! We've got fifty miles still to go. To-night we'll stay at a Moorhead hotel," Father said.

"Moorhead's a big place, isn't it?" Amory asked. "The hotel should have an elevator, just like Fargo, shouldn't it?" And Amory began to plan. "Perhaps if I rode on the elevator—"

Mother squelched his plan before he got any further. "Amory Johnston, I don't know what you're planning now, but you'll not go up or down in an elevator unless I'm with you."

When Lucy saw Gwen the next morning, waiting for them on the Maclarens' front steps, she saw her as the best friend anyone could have. When Gwen tumbled into the backseat, Lucy threw her arms around her so violently that the visor of Gwen's touring bonnet was permanently bent.

In no time at all, Gwen confessed she could hardly wait to get back to Wales. "All week I was running after somebody—all the time," Gwen reported. "Now I want to sit for a few days in our rocking chairs in the clubhouse."

"Me, too," echoed Lucy.

"You girls sound like a couple of old ladies," Mother said, laughing. "Rocking chairs at your age!"

Instead of driving west from Fargo, this time they drove north to Grand Forks, because Father wanted them to follow the prehistoric lake bed of that inland sea, Lake Agassiz. He first suggested that Mother unpack a suitcase and get out his geology book. When that suggestion didn't work, he began a lecture without the book.

"An inland sea—700 miles long, and very wide, too. Can't you see it, children? All that's left is this Red River of the North, running in this immense valley of the old lake. And the soil—richest in the world, I've heard."

Then he saw Amory was reading to himself in the new guidebook. So he looked for a moment to the backseat. There Lucy and Gwen were comparing the five rings from the Cracker Jack boxes, and Mother was sitting with a faraway gaze, as though she were still at the lake with her sisters.

"Even if you aren't interested in the past, you'd better look at your future. Pretty soon we'll be passing the University of North Dakota, and that's not prehistory—not yet," he said.

All day they rode, mostly going north, and only once did they lose their way. Mother's log was useless, since they weren't retracing their route. Amory read from the new guidebook. "Gumbo soil. Trail mark on post. Turn right." Then he shook his head. "Who wants to know it's gumbo? If it rains and you're stuck, you know that anyway. And there isn't even a post, so how can there be a trail mark?"

"We've been going west, haven't we?" Mother asked. "Where's your compass, Amory?"

"I lost it on the spider hunt, and I didn't think you'd want me to go back to all those places, so I'll just look for it next summer," Amory explained.

"We'll not be going again next summer. You know that, Armory." Mother spoke very firmly. "But right now, try to find something in the book that would tell us where we are."

But the book didn't help, and they sat, arguing about which way the trail should go, until Father said, "Let's get out of this buggy and stretch our legs."

Not far away was a clump of elms with some low bushes. "While we're here, Mother, I've just got to go into those bushes," Lucy said.

"All right. It may be a long time before we come to a real stop, especially since we don't know where we've stopped now," Mother answered in a discouraged tone.

As Lucy was coming back to the road, she tripped on a round stone. It turned over and tumbled her flat at the edge of the bushes. As she picked herself up, she saw at her feet an old fencepost so rotted at one end that it had toppled over. And on it were the faded black and white stripes that marked their trail.

"I've found it, and we aren't lost!" she shouted. "Here's where we turn right." They all hurried to check the post and the stripes and then the guidebook.

"You're a lucky girl," Father said, as they started off.

"Beautiful elms those were," Mother said, still looking back when the elms were only a fringe against the sky.

"But I can't wait to see our cottonwoods," Lucy said.

Father laughed. "There speaks our daughter of the prairie, Caroline."

That night they decided against another hotel and stayed in a house with a GUESTS sign. And compared to Claridge with all its hotel "extras," this clean little house, where the woman also cooked them a big breakfast, did make them feel like guests.

The last day was a day totally on the prairie, once they had climbed what Father called the Shelf, the old bank of the inland sea. Flat and large and wide, the prairie now spread out on either side of the dirt road, without a tree, without a hill, and only now and then the small dip of a coulee.

"I'd forgotten how it looks," said Gwen. "I like it, only it's different, isn't it?"

"Indeed it is," Mother answered. "Not a tree, not even a shrub—"

"But good soil and a good crop," Father interrupted.

"And look—millions of gophers! Does this place need a hunter!" Amory screeched.

On and on they went, with only two stops for flat tires. Lucy tried a pun about their tires getting "tired," but Father only gave her a look and said, "About time you took a turn pumping up this tube," and he handed her the pump.

By midafternoon they were in Langdon and drove at once to the front door of the Johnston cousins. To Lucy it was next best to being home in Wales again. Only Aunt Effie and Cousin Gen were there, but when Lucy opened the door to the kitchen, there was Gwin.

"Simply couldn't wait!" Gwin shouted, as she hugged everybody—that is, everybody but Amory. "We got home from Canada yesterday," Gwin kept on talking as she hugged. "And I had a toothache all night, and so Bill Bortz was driving down to get the Langdon doctor for his mother—and Lucy, look what I brought you." Gwin flung open the door to the shed and out sprang Topsy.

"Dear, dear Topsy," Lucy murmured, as she picked up her wriggling, yipping Topsy and hugged her tight, perhaps even tighter than she had hugged either of the Owens. After all, there were several Owens, but only one Topsy.

"I've been dressmaking while you were gone," Cousin Gen said, "so here's material for you girls to sew," and she handed over a heap of cloth that made the girls gasp.

"Caroline, put these three dozen fresh doughnuts in your picnic basket," Aunt Effie said, as they all piled back in the auto, Gwin and Topsy now making another layer on the backseat. "Amory, I see that basket is at your feet. You watch out," warned Aunt Effie. Again Lucy saw how well Aunt Effie understood boys and boys' feet, too.

On the ride home, Gwin never stopped talking, so they had all the village news before they saw the village. "Mrs. Bortz got bad news about her relatives in Germany and she was—well, Bill Bortz said she was 'took bad in the night,' so I don't know what's wrong. But he had to get the Langdon doctor because Dr. Carmer's away someplace getting cured of—well, getting cured, you know. And Charlie Dickerman's gained two pounds.

"And Great-aunt Maud gave our Edward a cricket bat to bring back so he could play a nice quiet English game, but yesterday while Mama was unpacking, he hit a Scheler on the head with it, and last night he batted Dorrie Flint on the backside and—"

"Hurrah for good old Edward," shouted Amory.

"And how's Guinnie?" asked Gwen, before Gwin began again.

"Oh, Guinnie went to tea so much with Mama that she wants us to have teas in the clubhouse and—"

"Gwinyth, could you stop talking for one minute?" Father asked. "If you don't give us a breather, I'm going to lose my way on the last five miles of our trip."

Gwin paused for half a minute, and then went on. "And Papa says Wales is better than he used to think. He says it's a good-hearted place, and maybe that's because the churchwomen sent in so much food that he's put on seven pounds and Mama may have to let out all his seams." Gwin halted, but since Father did nothing to stop her, she began again.

"And guess what! Papa heard that the young man the sheriff arrested is in the army now, fighting for the British Empire."

"Yes, I knew that a long time ago," Lucy said smugly.

"You did? And you never told us? How did you know?" Gwin was waiting for an answer.

But at that instant Amory caught sight of the six Wales elevators. "Wahooooo! Wahooooo! It's Wales!" he whooped.

There on the horizon were the six towers of their village, or so Lucy liked to think of them. And off at the right, at the Edge of Nowhere, stood the five tall cottonwoods.

"We're back!" Lucy sang out, and she turned to share the excitement with Mother beside her. But she noticed that Mother had tears behind her glasses. "Mother, you must be as glad to be home as I am. I could cry too, I'm so happy!" Lucy exclaimed.

Then Lucy gave a shout as loud as Amory's whoop —or louder.

"Home! We're home again! Dear old Wales!"